Win is the council assassins' handler, and that means he has to keep them safe. That's not an easy thing to do when there's a group of people trying to kill them, but Win has done his best, and now they're down to only six people to eliminate before he can take care of his family. But his obsession with their safety means he doesn't have time for anything else, and that includes Graham, the assassins' cook — and his mate.

Graham has suspected there was a bond between him and Win ever since he arrived at the warehouse, but since he's human, he can't be sure. He won't get any answers from Win, who spends more time in his office working than he should. If Graham wasn't there to make sure he ate and slept, he probably would have collapsed, and that's the last thing Graham wants.

Graham's opportunity to find out if that bond is really present comes when the council puts Win on a forced vacation. It so happens that Graham is headed home to his parents for two weeks, and somehow, Win ends up going with him. Will that interlude be enough for Graham to get through to Win? Or will Win be unable to forget about the work waiting for him back home and ignore Graham? Will the assassins finally find out what's really happening with the people trying to kill them?

Win
Copyright © 2019 Catherine Lievens
ISBN: 978-1-4874-2418-3
Cover art by Angela Waters

Published by eXtasy Books Inc or
Devine Destinies, an imprint of eXtasy Books Inc

Look for us online at:
www.eXtasybooks.com or www.devinedestinies.com

WIN
COUNCIL ASSASSINS BOOK 6

BY

CATHERINE LIEVENS

CHAPTER ONE

Win raked a hand through his hair and glared at the stack of documents on his desk. He'd already gone through them once, but he was going to have to do it again, just in case he'd missed anything. He wouldn't be surprised if he had, because he was having trouble seeing straight, and that meant he needed more coffee.

He got up and stretched, then rolled his neck. He wasn't sure how long he'd been sitting at his desk, but his leg was stiff, so it had been a while. That was nothing new, not since he'd become the handler for the council assassins. He loved his job and the people he protected and worked with, but he could have done without so much time in his chair.

He limped toward the small counter in the corner where the coffee pot was. The sludge left in the pot was cold and as black as tar, so he rinsed the pot in the sink and started a new one. He leaned against the counter as he waited, but his focus kept returning to the files on the desk.

He sighed. The council had already decided who the next assassins' targets would be in the list of people trying to kill them, so there wasn't much Win could do. He needed to, though. He felt like he wasn't doing enough to protect his family.

He just didn't have a clue *what* more to do.

He'd gone over all the files. He'd been in countless meetings with the council. He'd already picked who would have the marks based on what he knew about them. There wasn't anything else to do until his people came back from their job and told him if they'd found something new.

Because Win didn't believe that this was just a group of people trying to get rid of the council assassins and the council. There *had* to be more. He knew the council was a bother for a lot of powerful, rich people who wanted to do what they desired without having checks and balances and someone to answer to.

All the people on the list had money, so it might only be that they wanted more of it. But Win's instinct told him there was more to this. He just wasn't sure how to find it, and as far as he knew, there wasn't any hint of it in the files he already had. He hoped the assassins would be able to find out more after going on their next job, but there was no guaranteeing that, even though they had orders to interrogate their marks before killing them.

The knock on the door startled Win. He jumped and instantly berated himself for it. He eyed the door, wary. Was it Graham again? He wouldn't be surprised. The man had taken on the role of a mother hen with Win, and while Win's okapi was delighted at the attention and the closeness to their mate, Win's human side wasn't as happy. "Come in."

The door opened, and Beck peeked in. Win relaxed and waved him inside. Roark followed him, and Win realized it was already time for their meeting.

"Did you smell I was making fresh coffee?" he asked them, attempting humor.

Beck smiled, but Roark was staring at the files on Win's desk, and no doubt at the three empty coffee cups.

Win sighed. He wasn't in the mood for a scolding. He already got enough of that from Graham, even though he did his best to avoid the man.

"It doesn't look like you need more coffee," Roark pointed out.

"I'm not sure when I used those mugs, to be honest. They

could have been here since yesterday."

Roark arched a brow. "We both know that's bullshit. You're twitchy as fuck, Win."

Win glared. "You'd be twitchy in my place, too. It doesn't have anything to do with coffee."

"Not entirely, no, but the coffee isn't helping. Didn't Graham give you an herbal tea to drink or something?"

Win wrinkled his nose. "It smells like dirty socks." There was no way he was drinking that, not even because Graham had given it to him.

Beck flopped into one of the chairs in front of Win's desk. "The tea is that bad?"

"It stinks enough that I had to leave my office the one and only time I tried brewing it. I threw it away." Win paused. "But don't tell Graham that. He'd buy me another box."

Beck cocked his head. "Is that the only reason you don't want Graham to know?"

Damn it. Win knew people were curious about the way Graham and Win were behaving together. They were speculating and trying to get something out of him. Graham couldn't give them answers, since he was human, but Win knew they were mates. He realized he hadn't been as discreet as he should have been when he'd first met Graham. He probably still wasn't. But Graham was his mate, even though Win hadn't told him yet. He wanted to, but he had other things to focus on. He'd never forgive himself if something happened to one of the assassins because he'd been too distracted to focus on his job.

He huffed and poured himself a cup of coffee. Roark and Beck could get their own if they wanted to.

He shuffled to his side of the desk and sat, hoping he was able to hide that his leg hurt. He was spending too much time sitting in his chair lately. He needed to go to the gym and exercise, but again, there were more important things to do. "I asked you to come because I have the go-ahead of the council on the next targets."

He moved files around until he found the shortest list. He slid it toward Roark and Beck so they could read the names.

Roark picked it up. "Do they have a preference as to who is going after who?"

"No. They trust us to make that choice."

"Who are we sending?"

"I was thinking Heloise, Lawrence, and Armand, in that order. And the council has already told me they want to see me again, so I'm pretty sure they're going to give me another list soon. Hopefully at least one of the three will be back by then. I might have to send you, though, Roark, depending on who the council selects this time." The list of the people trying to kill the assassins wasn't infinite, but it was problematic.

There were several people on it whose death would be noticed, and that might create an uproar. That was one of the reasons the council was careful not to have everyone killed at the same time. Then, of course, there was the fact that they were trying to gather information. They had the list of the people who were in the group that wanted to get rid of the council, but Win wasn't the only one who thought there had to be more behind this. They were at a good point, but not everyone had been crossed off the list yet.

"Anything else?"

Win shook his head. "No. Beck?"

Beck sighed. "I already got through most of the computers we retrieved from the jobs. I haven't found anything new on those, and I'm still working on the last one I got. So far, nothing we didn't know yet."

Win rubbed his face. "All right. Hopefully, these three will give us more info."

"Are we sure there's more to it, though? I mean, yeah,

they're trying to kill the assassins to get to the council, but we've always known not everyone was happy with a council. A lot of shifters and whatnot didn't want to be regulated even in the beginning, and that hasn't changed over the years. Maybe they're really just trying to get rid of the council so they can go rogue again and do what they want."

Win tapped his fingertips on his desk. It was true that so far they hadn't found proof otherwise, but he was convinced there was more to it. Some of the people on the list, the people who wanted the council dead, were humans, and that didn't make sense. It was true that some humans dealt with the council, but they wouldn't be better off without it, not to the point that they'd get involved with a plot to kill the assassins and the council members.

He looked at Beck and Roark. "You might be right, but I don't want to leave anything out. Continue digging, and Roark and I will send Lawrence and the others on the jobs."

Beck nodded. "You need to rest, Win. You look like you're about to collapse."

"I'm fine."

"You don't look fine."

Win knew that Beck and the others cared about him as much as he cared about them, but he wished they didn't. He was overworking himself for their safety, and he wasn't sure they understood that. If they did, they didn't seem to want him to, but there was no way he was backing down, not on this.

He was going to make sure all the members of his family were safe and sound by the time this was over, even if it killed him.

Graham stirred the onions, careful not to let them burn. He could do this in his sleep, but he was distracted enough that he wanted to be sure. Of course, he'd been distracted since he'd arrived, so maybe he was better at this than he thought.

Damn Win and his stubbornness. Graham didn't get it, and he wasn't sure what to do about it. He liked Win and how caring he was, but that same care was the main obstacle between them.

There wasn't a *them*, though. Win never gave Graham the time of day. He kept Graham at arm's length, even though Graham could swear that sometimes, Win looked at him like he wanted him. It didn't happen often, only when Win was tired and vulnerable, but Graham knew what he'd seen, and he wanted to see it more often.

He wanted Win, period. But he didn't know how to get him.

He'd tried everything. He took care of Win when everyone else stayed back. He made sure Win ate and slept enough, even though Win fought him every step of the way. He talked to Win, but Win didn't answer most of the time, as if he wasn't listening. Graham knew he was, though, because sometimes he mentioned those conversations. But short of being straightforward and asking Win what the fuck his problem was, Graham didn't know what to do. Maybe he *should* do that. He'd been tempted more than once, but what if he scared Win into running even more?

Something poked Graham in the side. He jerked and held his wooden spoon up to hit whatever it was. He managed to stop himself in time before hitting Milo's arm, and he glared at him. "What the fuck, Milo?"

Milo raised his hands. "I just wanted to make sure you wouldn't burn dinner because you were daydreaming about Win."

Graham stuck his tongue out. "Who said I was thinking about him? Maybe I finally decided to move on to one of the other single guys who live here. Ulric is cute."

Milo's gaze held pity, and Graham hated it. "Come on. We both know you're crushing on Win hard enough that you can't move on."

Graham didn't want to confirm that, and he didn't need to. He turned his attention back on the onions in the pot and noticed they were done. He added the mushrooms and continued stirring, hoping Milo would stop looking at him.

He didn't.

Ever since Milo had met his mate, he was sticking his nose into Graham's business. Graham knew it was because he wanted him to be as happy as he was. And while he loved Milo for that, he wished his best friend would focus on his mate rather than on him.

Milo sighed and leaned against the counter where he could watch Graham even though Graham faced the stove. "Why are you so focused on him?" he asked.

Graham snorted. "Don't you think I've asked myself that a hundred times already? I don't know, Milo. I just . . . want him. There's no explanation. He's a nice guy. He cares about his people, makes sure everyone is all right and has everything they need. He focuses on them even when it's bad for him and his health. He's self-sacrificing, something that makes me mad as much as it makes me like him." Graham smiled. He always did when he thought about Win. "I just can't ignore him, even when he's not there."

"You know what that sounds like, right?"

"Like I'm crazy about a guy who hasn't looked at me twice?" Because no matter how much Graham hoped, he wasn't a fool. It was obvious that while Win was grateful for the food he gave him and everything else, he was doing his best to ignore Graham, and Graham wasn't sure how long he could do this. He wasn't going anywhere, but maybe he should stop putting his heart on the line for a guy who couldn't care less about him.

Milo leaned closer. "It sounds like a mate bond to me, Graham."

Graham shook his head. He didn't want to contemplate that option. He didn't want to think about why Win was avoiding him so often if they were mates. "I don't think that's it."

"You can't know unless you ask him, though, right? You're human."

"I'm aware of that."

"You should talk to him."

"Don't you think I haven't tried?" Graham put his spoon down and grabbed the patties he'd put together earlier. It took him a moment to put all of them into the pan because there were so many of them. He supposed he should be glad Win and the council had installed a kitchen that looked like it belonged in a restaurant, pots and pans included. Some of them were big enough that he could cook for everyone in only two waves.

Milo patted Graham's shoulder. "I know you have. But if you and Win are mates, don't you think you owe it to yourself to try again and again until you get an answer from him?"

"Maybe." Graham knew he did. He wouldn't be able to let go until he knew for sure if Win wanted him or not.

Maybe Milo was right, and they *were* mates. Graham knew there was something about Win, whatever it was, that made it impossible for him to forget him. He wouldn't be able to even if they didn't both live in the warehouse. He'd never been so focused and obsessed with a guy, though. He didn't know if it was because there was something special about Win or because they were mates, but he wanted to find out.

"This isn't the best moment to bug him," he said.

Milo grimaced. "That's true. But I'm not sure there'll ever

be a good moment. I mean, I've lived here for as long as you have, so I can't be sure, but something tells me there's always another job, another danger this family has to face."

"Probably, but I doubt it's as dangerous as it is now. It's the first time the assassins are personally targeted, right?"

Milo bit his lower lip. His mate, North, was an assassin, and that put him right in the middle of danger. Graham hated to remind him of that, although he doubted Milo ever stopped thinking about it. He knew he didn't, even though Win never went out on jobs. He was the handler, and he spent his time between the warehouse and the council's offices, wherever they were.

But he was still a part of this group, and that meant his life was in danger every single minute of every day, just like everyone else's was. The fear and worry that tugged on Graham's stomach were hard to ignore sometimes.

The door to the stairs opened, and several people came in. Graham forced himself to smile at them, even though after his chat with Milo, he felt like doing anything but smile.

"Smells good! What's for dinner?" Lawrence asked.

Ulric made a beeline for the stove like he always did, and Graham fended him off with his spoon. Ulric's heartbroken expression made Graham smile, and it was a little easier to forget about Win's rejection. "Stay away from my pans," he warned Ulric.

"But I'm hungry."

"You're *always* hungry," Payne said, leaning over to peek into the pan.

Graham huffed. "You all need to back off and let me finish this. And it's Salisbury steak."

"Mmm, mushrooms," Ulric said. He tried to sneak past Graham again, and Graham arched a brow at him. Ulric pouted. "I just wanted a taste."

"I know. You can get one once we're all ready to sit down.

Why don't you set the table in the meantime?" Sometimes, dealing with the assassins was like dealing with kids. It was an odd conundrum, but Graham liked it. It made them seem more human, and it was easy to forget what they did for a living.

Ulric sighed dramatically. "All right. But you should re-think that date with me. I can beg."

Graham laughed. "You only want me because I'm a cook."

Ulric grinned. "Well, yeah. Why else would I want to be with anyone?"

Graham wasn't hurt by Ulric's joking around. He knew there was more to the man than his stomach and that he cared for him. Besides, Ulric wasn't Graham's type. No, his type ran more to brooding, limping men who didn't look at him twice.

The door opened again, and Graham looked up, hoping to see Win. Of course, it wasn't him. Beck smiled at Graham and sniffed. "Smells good."

Graham cleared his throat. "It's almost ready. Is Win coming up to eat with us?"

Beck frowned. "I doubt it. He was working again when we left his office."

Of course he was. Knowing him, Graham doubted he'd had breakfast. That meant Graham was going to have to take him a plate.

He didn't mind.

The words danced in front of Win's eyes. He supposed that was a sign he wasn't sleeping enough. Or maybe it was the coffee? Whatever he'd told Beck and Roark, four coffees before lunchtime was a bit much, even for him. But he needed it to keep going, so he got up to get a fifth cup. There was no more space for his mug on the desk, and he had to pick up the four empty ones. He put them into the sink and went back to the desk, snatching his phone to call Kameron Rhett, one of the council members, to tell him he'd selected the assassins for the next jobs.

A knock on the door interrupted him before he could dial the number. He sighed, hoping it wasn't Roark with yet another problem they needed to solve. "Yes?" he called out.

The door opened, and of course, since Win had shitty luck, Graham walked in. Win almost groaned in dismay, but he managed to keep the sound in. It was especially easy because Graham was holding a plate with food that smelled divine, and it made Win's stomach growl.

Graham must have heard it — he smiled. "I knew you'd be hungry."

Win was, but he wasn't going to admit that. He didn't want to give Graham an inch. It would be all too easy to let him in if he did. Graham was already doing a good job burrowing under Win's skin as he was. "I'm not."

"Your stomach says otherwise." Graham came closer to the desk and tsked. "Where am I supposed to put this? Come on. Move those files."

"Graham—" Win didn't want to spend time alone with him, not any more than he already had. Graham hadn't asked him anything about them yet, but he was bound to sooner or later. Win knew he was lucky that for now, he hadn't. He wouldn't be lucky for much longer, not if he knew Graham — and he did, kind of.

He might stay away from his mate as much as he could, but that didn't mean he didn't look at him, that he didn't observe him. It made him feel like a creep most of the time, but it was all he could allow himself to have with Graham for now, and it had to be enough.

Graham was a good man. He cared for the assassins even

knowing what they were and what they did. He'd fit right in when he'd arrived even though he didn't have a mate in the warehouse.

Not that he knew of, anyway.

Win realized he was going to have to talk to Graham sooner or later, and he anticipated that moment as much as he dreaded it. He wanted Graham in his life, and he'd have to tell him that if he asked, but he needed to focus on saving his family first. Once everyone was safe and he didn't have to worry about them more than usual, he'd allow himself to talk to Graham.

Of course, that would only work if Graham stayed away, something he didn't seem to be inclined to do.

Graham arched a brow. "Nope. Don't *Graham* me. You need to eat, and I have food. I know you didn't have break-fast, so don't even try to tell me you're not hungry again. Come on. Get those files off the desk before I plonk this plate on top of them. You know I'll do it."

Win did. He huffed and puffed as he stacked the files on one side of the desk. Graham wasn't wrong—he needed to eat. He didn't feel well, and he *was* hungry.

He knew he was neglecting himself and that it wouldn't end well for him if he weren't careful. He just needed to do *more*. He didn't know how, but he'd find a way, and that didn't include spending time with Graham and telling him they were mates or begging him to bond with Win.

"There." The plate clunked on the desk when Graham set it down. He leaned closer and wrinkled his nose at Win's cup. "What number is that?"

"What?"

"The coffee. Wait, let me guess? Number three?"

Win glared. "It's my fourth, and it's none of your busi-ness. Thank you for the meal, Graham. You can go now."

Graham ignored Win. He grabbed the mug instead and

brought it to the sink, where he threw out its contents.

"Graham!" Win barked.

Graham didn't even look at him. He emptied the coffee pot into the sink, too, and turned the water on. He got a fork and a knife out of the drawer and took them over to Win's desk, depositing them next to the plate. Then he went back to the sink and washed the mugs.

Win couldn't look away from him. Graham was taking care of him even though he didn't know they were mates. There was no way he could, since he was human, although sometimes, Win wondered. Being human didn't mean he didn't feel anything. Humans felt the bond, too. It wasn't as strong for them, but there was no denying it. Was that the reason Graham kept coming back even though Win did his best to push him away?

Probably, and there was nothing Win could do about it. He couldn't change the fact that they were mates. He didn't want to. He wanted Graham in his life, just not right now. And he knew he owed it to Graham to talk to him and to tell him the truth, to explain what was going on, but he couldn't. It would take too much time from him, too much attention he needed to dedicate to finding the assholes who wanted to kill his family.

So he kept his mouth shut, at least when it came to talking. He did eat Graham's food, though. It was delicious, just like always.

And as he ate, he watched Graham.

Once Graham was done washing the mugs and the coffee machine, he wiped down the counter and the cupboards. He put everything away, and Win didn't miss that he didn't put on a new pot of coffee. It didn't matter. Win would make one as soon as Graham was gone.

"Oh, I didn't give you anything to drink. Sorry," Graham said. He opened the fridge, and even though he was at his desk, Win saw him wrinkle his nose. "Soda? Come on, Win. Don't you get enough caffeine in your coffee? Where's that herbal tea I gave you?"

Win had thrown it away, but he wasn't about to confess that, not to Graham. "I drank it."

Graham grabbed a bottle of water and closed the fridge. "All of it? Really?"

"Really."

"And you expect me to believe that?"

Win pressed his lips together. He couldn't smile. "I can't tell you what to believe or not, but it's the truth. Don't you have something better to do, Graham? Have you eaten, or did you come down here before eating?"

Graham put the bottle in front of Win. "I'll eat later. I have to cook a second time anyway, so don't worry about me."

Win looked down. "I'm not worried about you."

"Of course you're not. Drink that water, Win. The entire bottle. It'll do you better than another pot of coffee. And if you don't slow down on that, I'll take your grounds away."

Win leaned back in his chair and crossed his arms over his chest. "You realize you can't order me around, right? I'm the boss here."

"Yeah, yeah." Graham straightened the pile of files on the edge of Win's desk. "Finish your dinner, Win."

"I can finish it as easily if you leave."

Graham smiled at Win, and Win fell in love with him a little bit more. "I'm not going anywhere, so stop trying to make me leave. I'll go once you're done eating."

Win knew he wouldn't get anything else out of Graham. Win was stubborn, but so was Graham, and especially when it came to Win. Win supposed it was the bond again.

He wasn't sure how he was going to deal with it if Graham continued to act like this. It was becoming harder and harder to resist him, and Win suspected that one day, he'd stop trying and give in.

Graham didn't like what he was seeing. Win always looked tired, but today was worse. He had dark circles under his eyes, and if Graham wasn't mistaken, he'd lost weight. He couldn't afford to lose weight, because he was so skinny to begin with. It couldn't be good for his health, not when he wasn't eating.

Graham's chest warmed when Win went back to eating. He wasn't sure how warm the food was by now, but he wasn't about to ask Win if he wanted it warmed. He didn't want to interrupt, not when he finally had what he wanted.

Or part of what he wanted, because it was obvious Win needed sleep as much as he needed food. Graham wasn't going to leave him a choice in this. Once Win was done, he was dragging his ass to bed.

Graham sighed. He wished he could get into that bed with Win, but he'd be happy enough if Win just went to sleep. One day, he'd bring the conversation up with Win, and he'd get the answers he wanted almost as much as he wanted Win. Today was not that day, though, and he doubted tomorrow would be, either. Win was completely focused on saving the assassins from the people after them, as was right.

"I promise I'll eat even if you leave," Win said.

It was a pretty desperate attempt to get Graham to leave, and Graham just smiled at him. Win scowled, but he continued eating until his fork scraped on the plate. He gathered as much gravy as he could, and Graham made sure he wasn't beaming like a fool when Win looked at him again.

"See? It wasn't that hard," he said.

Win scowled. "I never said it was hard. I just don't have

time to waste."

"Eating is *not* wasting time. You're going to faint sooner or later if you don't take better care of yourself, and where would that leave everyone? You can't help them if you're not conscious."

"I'm fine," Win groused.

That was what he always said, though, and Graham suspected he'd say it until he was found unconscious on the floor. That was, if someone actually found him before he woke up. He spent so much time holed up alone in his office that not finding him was a real possibility.

Graham took the plate from Win's desk and smiled at him. "You ate everything."

Win shrugged and looked away. "I might have been hungrier than I thought."

"That's good." Graham put the plate into the small sink. "All right. Let's go."

Win frowned. "What?"

"You're going to bed, and you're going now."

"I can't. I have more work to do."

"Work that will still be there when you wake up tomorrow morning. When was the last time you slept eight hours? Hell, when was the last time you slept six hours? And six hours aren't nearly enough, by the way, but I'd be surprised if you even slept that every night."

"You're not my doctor."

Graham grinned. "You're right, I'm not, but I do know your doctor, and I won't have a problem telling him about this. I bet he'd be interested in listening to me."

"I forbid you to do that."

Graham put his hands on his hips and arched a brow. "Oh, you *forbid* me to do it? Win, I'm not one of your assassins. I don't obey your orders."

"I'm the one who employs you."

"No, you're not. The council employs me. You can't even fire me, not unless you give the council a good reason to. And before you say it, I know you could come up with something. You won't."

"You sound sure of that."

"It's because I am." Graham smiled even more widely. He liked this banter with Win. It gave him a new look into Win's personality. He didn't know him well beyond the worry he had for everyone in the warehouse and the fact that he worked a lot. "I know you like me, and even if you didn't, you'd have a revolt on your hands if you tried to fire me. Everyone here loves my food, and I doubt they want to go back to bland pasta and burned chicken."

A flash of amusement passed in Win's gaze, enough that Graham knew he wasn't angry. He wasn't smiling, but then, he didn't smile often.

Graham was going to change that, somehow.

He walked to the desk and took Win's hand, hoping Win wouldn't push him away. "Come on."

Win's eyes widened, and to Graham's surprise, he got up. "Where are we going?"

"To bed."

Win looked stunned.

Graham grinned. "I meant that I was putting you to bed. I have to go cook again and eat. But I'll check in on you to make sure you're asleep later." Graham doubted it would take Win more than a few minutes to fall asleep. He was exhausted, no matter how much he tried to deny it, even to himself.

"I don't need you to check on me. I'm not a child. And I need to work."

"I know, I know. But like I said, your work will still be there tomorrow, and I doubt the people you work with are as dedicated as you are. They're probably all having dinner or even an early night right now. Come on, Win. You'll feel better after a good night's sleep, and you'll be able to think better, too. You haven't made mistakes yet, but it's bound to happen if you don't give yourself time to rest. It's not wasted time, you know. It's time invested so you can work better and protect everyone to the best of your ability, without exhaustion weighing you down." Graham pulled. "Come on."

He was only mildly surprised when Win came along. He'd expected him to protest harder. Probably it was a sign of how tired Win was. No matter how much he denied it, he had to know it wouldn't do anyone any good for him to insist on doing this.

Graham hoped the people still in the kitchen and in the living room wouldn't say anything when they saw them. They all liked to tease, but that was the last thing Win needed right now.

Graham glared at the usual suspects as soon as he stepped foot into the kitchen. Armand snapped his mouth shut, but his eyes were twinkling, and Graham knew he'd take shit from him later. He didn't care, not as long as he got Win into bed without anyone yapping their big mouth.

Graham didn't hesitate to push the door to Win's bedroom open. He'd been there before, mostly when he forced Win to get some sleep. He hated that it was the only reason, but they'd get there. He had to believe that.

Win freed his hand, but if he thought Graham was going to leave without making sure he was in bed, he was wrong. Graham gently pushed him onto the bed and, ignoring Win's wide eyes, knelt in front of him. He took Win's shoes and socks off, dumping them to the floor.

"What are you doing?" Win asked. His voice was little more than a whisper.

"I'm making sure you're comfortable."

"You don't have to do that."

"I want to, Win. Just let me do this for you. I *like* taking care of you." Graham rose. He hesitated, wondering if Win would allow him to take the next step. There was so much that was unsaid between them, but Graham knew they belonged together. He just needed Win to let go and admit it. "Stretch out."

Win licked his lips. "What are you doing?"

"You can't sleep in jeans. You'd be uncomfortable."

"I can take them off myself."

"I know you can. Let me take care of you, Win. You don't allow anyone close to you. I'm not asking for much, just . . . let me do this, please." Graham *needed* to take care of Win. He didn't know why, and he didn't want to examine that feeling right now. He wasn't ready for what it might mean, for what any of this might mean.

He thought Win was going to tell him to fuck off, but to his surprise, he slowly reclined instead. His cheeks were flushed, and he wasn't looking at Graham, not even when Graham quickly unfastened his jeans and slid them down his legs.

There was nothing sexual about it, and Graham made sure not to turn the situation into that. He could tell Win was self-conscious from how fast he slid under the covers, and that was okay. But Graham wanted him to know he didn't care. "You don't have to hide," he whispered as he tucked Win in.

"I don't know what you're talking about."

"Of course you don't. Still. I don't care about your leg or whatever scars you're hiding. You're beautiful, Win, and you should know that. It's a pity no one else ever tells you that." But if Graham got what he wanted, he'd be the one to tell Win for the rest of their lives.

CHAPTER TWO

W in needed to stop thinking about Graham. He knew that. He'd tried to.

But he was still thinking about him. He couldn't focus on anything else. His mind kept on going back to that evening a few days before. Graham had taken care of Win like no one had in a long time. Win realized it was his fault. He didn't let anyone close, not the way he'd allowed Graham. He shouldn't have, though. It was making it harder to keep Graham at arm's length.

But Win had to. He had to focus on his job, on keeping his family safe, and he couldn't do that if he kept thinking about Graham.

He shook his head and checked the time. He'd wasted half an hour staring at the wall and thinking about Graham, which meant he had to go if he didn't want to be late for his meeting with the council. He was supposed to report the progress they were making on shortening the list of the people trying to kill them. He could have done without having to do it every week, but he understood why the council wanted him to. Their lives were on the line, too, and they were much more important than the assassins who were in charge of protecting them and making sure they could do their jobs.

At least not the entire council would be there. Win supposed he should consider himself lucky. Not all the council members thought he should be doing this job. They had several reasons for that—his bum leg, of course, but also the fact

that he wasn't a predator shifter. Most of them were sup-
portive, and since they'd held a vote when he'd been offered
the job, Win wasn't about to lose it. That didn't mean it was
easy to face those few people who thought he shouldn't be
there.

They were already there when he got to the building
where they met. He waved Dasha off and straightened, hoping the fact that his leg hurt wasn't obvious. He didn't want
to give the people who didn't like him yet another reason to
try to get him fired from the job.

"Relax," Nysys whispered when Win passed him by.
"The assholes aren't here today."

Win pressed his lips together. He didn't want to be disre-
spectful, or even to appear that he was.

Dominic, who was sitting next to Nysys, snorted. "You
know, Nysys, sometimes I wish you didn't live at the mansion with the pride, but then you redeem yourself this way."
He grinned at Win. "And he's right. The assholes aren't here
today. Sit down, Win."

Win obeyed, grateful. His leg ached, but then it always
did. That didn't mean he couldn't do his job, though.
"There's not much to say yet," he said, warning the people
present.

"But I *live* for our meetings," Nysys crowed.

Win rolled his eyes and ignored him. He wasn't sure who
had thought that making Nysys a council member was a
good idea, although he was glad for his presence. He always
managed to make things lighter and nicer.

"Like I said, there's nothing much to talk about yet. I sent
three assassins on their jobs. One of them has already re-
turned. Unfortunately, or maybe not, the man he was sent to
take care of had a heart attack. That means he didn't have
the time to interrogate him. We have the man's computer,
though, and Beck is already digging through it." Win cleared

his throat. "And that brings me to one of my problems. I know we shouldn't bring new people in right now, not with this hanging over our heads, but I need more tech people. Beck is great at what he does, but he's only one man, and it's not enough."

Kameron rubbed the back of his neck. "You're right on both counts. I suppose we could hire someone and make sure no one finds out about it, but I'm not sure who we can trust. I'm not even sure I trust all the council members most days."

That wasn't something Win had considered, although he knew he should have. He looked around the table. It could be personal bias, but he trusted everyone there—Dominic, Kameron, Nysys, Quincy, and Cole. "Do you really think a council member is behind this?"

"I don't want to think so, but how can we be sure when we haven't gotten to the bottom of it? But if you can find someone willing to start working with us and stick to the warehouse, let us know. We can vet them and see if it's possible."

Win had already asked Beck for a list of people he knew were as good as he was and who would be willing to work with them. He'd just been waiting for the council's approval to start going through their background and contacting them. "I'll see what I can do."

"What about the other two targets?" Dominic asked. Nysys was doodling on a piece of paper and looking like he wasn't listening, but Win knew better.

"Still on them. I'll contact you as soon as I have news."

Nysys looked up. "Are we done? Because I'm hungry."

Win smiled. He couldn't *not* smile at Nysys most of the time. "I don't have anything else to say right now." Which was why he'd wanted to wait to have this meeting, but he wasn't the one who made the decisions here.

Nysys pushed his chair away. "Great! See you when I see you." He waved and left the room without looking back. Win chuckled. That was typical Nysys. He always smiled, even when things were dire. They weren't, not as much as they'd been before, but it still wasn't a walk in the park.

"Well, we're going, too," Quincy said as he and Cole got up.

Win gathered the files he'd brought with him and handed them to Quincy, who nodded in thanks. He'd make sure to give them to the other council members who hadn't been there.

Win leaned back in his chair and rubbed his forehead. He had the beginning of a headache, probably because he hadn't eaten breakfast, and because for the first time in forever, he'd slept more than five hours. That had been thanks to Graham, although right now, Win wished he hadn't forced him to go to sleep. He didn't have the time to deal with a headache right now.

"Are you okay?"

Win blinked up at Kameron. The alpha was leaning over him, a frown on his face. Win hated when people worried about him, so he nodded and got up. "Of course."

"You look tired."

Dominic snorted. "He looks dead on his feet."

"That's true. Did you have breakfast this morning?"

Win huffed. "Why does everyone worry about how much I eat?"

"I didn't know someone else was worried, but I'm going to go out on a limb and guess they care about you."

"As do we," Kameron added. "Come on, let's go to lunch."

Again, why the fuck was everyone so worried about Win's eating habits? "I have to go back to my office. I have work to do."

"And you'll go back—after lunch. Look, we need to eat, you need to eat, and from what I know about you, you usually have sandwiches at your desk, if you don't forget to eat period."

That was exactly how things had been before Graham. Now that he was there, he made sure Win had at least one hot meal every day and that he went to bed at a decent hour. Win would probably have been offended and angry if Graham hadn't been his mate, but as it was, he loved that Graham wanted to take care of him. Even though Graham didn't know they were mates, he worried, and Win couldn't remember the last time someone had.

Dominic hooked his arm under Win's and pulled him toward the door. "Whatever you have waiting for you at your office can wait. Let's go eat lunch, talk about whatever you want, although I'd rather not talk about this fucking mess we're in again. We're friends, yeah?"

Win had never thought of the council members that way, but it was true he was close to some of them, including Kameron and Dominic. "I guess."

Dominic pressed his palm against his chest. "I'm wounded. We'll talk about that while we're eating. You need to realize you're not an island."

"He's too thin to be one," Kameron intervened.

Why was Win friends with these guys again?

"What about this?" Lawrence asked. He was holding a packet of ready-to-eat rice.

Graham wrinkled his nose. "If you want rice, tell me, and I'll cook it for you. But there won't be any of that stuff in my house."

Lawrence grinned. "You're snobbish. I hadn't realized that."

"I'm not snobbish. I just don't want to feed you guys trash."

Lawrence looked at the rice. "It's not trash."

"Maybe not, and I'm sure it's convenient for people who don't have a cook living with them at home, but you do, so put it down, and never look at it again, please."

"You heard the man," Dasha said. *He* was holding a bag of chocolate, and Graham glared at him. Dasha grinned and put the chocolate into his basket. "What? I like chocolate, and you don't make it."

Graham probably could, but he was more a cook than a baker. "Fine. Take the chocolate."

Sometimes, he hated having to go food shopping with guards. He understood why it was necessary, though, and he was grateful that the people who came with him always managed to make things fun and make him forget why they were there. At least this time they were only buying a few odds and ends. The last time they'd gone to buy in bulk, he'd lost track of one of his bodyguards, and it had taken him almost an hour to find him.

Lawrence put down the rice. "Fine. But I want chocolate, too."

"You're going to have to go get it yourself," Dasha warned him.

"I will." Lawrence leaned his hip against the cart and almost fell on his face when it moved.

Graham rolled his eyes and dumped a big bag of rice — *not* the ready-to-eat kind — into the cart.

"So, Graham," Lawrence began.

Graham knew from his tone that he wasn't going to like what was next. "What?" he asked, wary.

"You and Win, huh?"

And there it was. How was Graham supposed to answer that? He and Win weren't together. He wasn't even sure they were friends, but he knew Lawrence wouldn't take that for an answer. Graham could tell him to fuck off, because it was none of his business, and Lawrence wouldn't push, but Graham needed friends. Maybe having more people knowing how he felt about Win would help. Milo had made his opinion clear, but Graham still wasn't sure talking to Win was a good idea, not right now.

On the other hand, what would Win think if he knew Graham was spreading their business around? He considered the assassins his family, but he always kept himself separate from them, probably because in a way, he was their boss. Would he have a problem with Graham telling them about him?

"You have a crush on him," Lawrence said. It wasn't a question, so Graham ignored him and pushed the cart away.

"Come on," Lawrence said. "You can tell me. And Dasha, too. We promise not to tell anyone."

"What's it to you if I do?" Graham asked. He could tell Lawrence and Dasha about that, make it sound one-sided. He wasn't sure it wasn't, though. Of course, he also wasn't sure it was, so what did he know?

"Nothing. We all want Win to be happy, though."

"That's why you're sticking your nose into it?"

"I'm not sticking my nose into anything. I just want to be encouraging." Lawrence shrugged. "Win is like . . . I don't know . . . not a father figure, but definitely a big brother, at least to me. We can all see he's not okay. He's obsessed with making sure we're safe, and that's great, but it's not all there is to life. Everyone else has other people and things to focus on, but he doesn't. It would be nice to see him happy, and if it's with you, that's even better."

Graham smiled. "I'm pretty sure I annoy him."

"That's because you make him realize that he can't take care of everything and that he's not taking care of himself.

You force him to take a step back."

Graham knew that was true. He still didn't want to talk about it, but knowing that people could see there was something between him and Win and that they approved made him feel better. Now he just had to make Win see that, too.

They could be good together. Graham wanted to take care of Win forever, to make sure he ate and slept enough, that he didn't kill himself with work. No one else seemed to care, although he knew that wasn't true. He was the only one ready to push, though. The others worried, but like Lawrence had said, they had other things to focus on — their job, their mate.

And Graham had Win.

"We just wanted you to know," Dasha murmured. "Now come along, Law. Let's get you that chocolate."

Lawrence grinned. "Great."

"Grab some for me, too!" Graham yelled after them.

For all that his job wasn't an easy one because he had to cook every day for a lot of people and he was far from his family, he loved what he did. He loved the people he lived and worked with, and that more than made up for the difficulties. Still, he was glad he had two weeks of vacation coming up. He needed to get out of the warehouse for a bit, and maybe spending time away from Win would help him see things more objectively.

Graham wasn't sure how much more he could tolerate without talking to Win and telling him everything — that he loved him, that he worried about him, and that he wanted them to be together. That he needed Win to take better care of himself because he worried.

Graham couldn't stop thinking about it as he, Lawrence, and Dasha shimmered home with the groceries. He didn't have to think to cook lunch, and he let the familiar movements soothe him.

Win was asking too much of himself and his body. Sooner or later, he was going to break. Graham hoped the people trying to get the council and their assassins killed would get caught soon, but there was no way to be sure of that, and even if they were, who was to say there weren't more people behind it? Graham wasn't an assassin, but he listened to their conversations. He knew they suspected there was something more behind this than just killing the assassins. They didn't know what it was yet, and that was terrifying, because how could they stop the madness?

Even if they killed all the people in the group against the council, the situation would still be what it was. They would still be in danger, and Win would still obsess over keeping everyone safe and working until he collapsed. All the others had relaxed, albeit slightly, but he hadn't, and it worried Graham to no end.

Maybe he should talk to Rocco about it. He had a hard time believing the doctor hadn't noticed, so he hoped it meant he wasn't worried, but then, he wasn't in love with Win. Graham didn't want to break Win's trust, so the doctor was probably out, even if only for suggestions. Maybe Graham could continue the way he was, making sure Win ate and slept. It wasn't perfect, but it would be better than nothing, and at least that way Win didn't protest too much.

Win wasn't there when the others sat at the table, of course. Graham put a plate together to take it downstairs, but Roark's voice stopped him. "He's not here."

Graham blinked. "No?"

"He had a meeting with the council today. He should have been back already, but maybe things got more complicated than he expected. I'm sure he'll be back soon, though. You should put that plate in the microwave."

Graham knew better. Even if he did what Roark suggested and put the plate away, there was no way Win would come upstairs to eat. He'd probably hole up in his office as soon as he came back. He always did.

"Is everything okay?" Graham asked Roark.

"I'm sure it is. He hasn't called me, but sometimes these meetings go long. Maybe some council member has some info they want to share or something. But don't worry. Win will call me if something happens, and I'll let you know."

Graham nodded. He wrapped the plate and put it away. He'd take it downstairs after lunch to leave it on Win's desk. He hoped it would be an obvious sign that he wanted Win to eat it, and that Win would obey the silent order.

He knew Graham would come after him if he didn't.

Win leaned back in his chair and smiled. He hadn't expected to have so much fun at lunch, since he, Kameron, and Dominic weren't exactly friends. They worked together and respected each other, but it was obvious the other two men shared more than that. The fact that they had included Win in their conversation made him feel warm.

And of course, they both had fun stories to share. Win wasn't surprised that Nysys managed to be so chaotic, and he was planning to tease him the next time they saw each other.

"I'm telling you," Dominic said. "I beg Morin at least once a week to move both of them to New York."

Kameron chuckled. "Isn't that where they already live?"

"It was supposed to be, but Nysys spends more time at the mansion than in his apartment, to the point that he and Morin have their own room. I swear, Nysys likes to say he lives in New York, but he really doesn't."

"I hope for your sake he never has kids. Can you imagine what *that* would be like?"

"Good Lord. With my luck, he'd have twins or something, and then I'd have three of them causing chaos."

"But I bet your kid would love it."

Dominic's smile softened. "He would. Although Nysys is inappropriate most of the time, he's a great uncle, and he loves all the children in the mansion."

Win squirmed in his chair. He didn't talk about kids, mostly because he didn't have any, and neither did anyone in the warehouse. It wasn't a place for children, and Win had thought about it long and hard before allowing Greg and Payne to stay with them. Of course, that had ended up being a good thing, since Greg was Evan's mate, but the responsibility had still terrified Win, and they'd both been teenagers. He could only imagine what he'd do if someone gave him a baby to hold.

"How's Zach?" Dominic asked.

"He's doing great. I think he wants another baby, though. The twins are grown now."

Win sighed. Did Graham want children? Had he ever thought about it? Probably, since he was human, and they didn't have as much time as shifters to make that kind of decision. What if he did, though? Could Win give him that?

Once Win had accepted his job as the assassins' handler, he hadn't thought he'd ever do anything else. Of course, he'd realized that some, if not most, of the assassins would eventually retire like Roark had. He was lucky Roark had decided to stick around and help him handle the others, but sooner or later, one of them was bound to decide he wanted to cut away from this life.

What if Graham was that person? What if he decided that before Win was ready to talk to him about them?

"What about you, Win?" Kameron asked, jerking Win out of his thoughts. "Do you have a girlfriend? Boyfriend?"

Win *hated* being the center of attention. "No."

"Why not?"

"There's no time for that, especially not now that I have to make sure everyone at the warehouse is safe." He shrugged. "That takes precedence, and I doubt a lot of people would understand that. And of course, there's the fact that my job is what it is. Who would want to get into that kind of situation?"

Kameron arched a brow. "Seems to me a lot of people don't mind. How many of your guys are mated now?"

Win groaned. "Tell me about it. It's all love and little birds at home some days."

"Maybe you'll find your mate, too. And hey, since mates are perfect for us, they probably won't care about what you do and where you live. The ones who live with you don't seem to, like I said."

Win hesitated. He wasn't friends with Kameron and Dominic, but then, he wasn't friends with anyone. He was a boss, a big brother kind of guy, the one who made sure everyone was all right and taken care of, that they were careful when they went out for jobs. He loved the people he lived with, considered them his family, but the fact that he was kind of their boss meant he'd always kept himself slightly apart.

So he was always apart—except with Graham. With him, Win felt like he belonged, like he could be himself. And he supposed he could. They were mates, and that meant something. Of course, it would mean more if Win could actually do something about it, but it was too soon. It wasn't the right time, not when he still had to focus on taking out the people planning to kill them.

"You can tell us." Dominic leaned forward. "I realize we're not friends, but we're in a similar position. You're not an alpha, but you *are* in charge of the assassins, and it's always a complicated position. You're their friend, their family, but you're also the boss. It's not an easy thing to balance.

That's one of the reasons Kameron and I are friends. It's easier because we're both alphas."

Fuck. Win wanted to talk about Graham. He wanted to gush about his mate, to tell everyone how good a cook he was, how caring he was.

He cleared his throat. "There *is* someone."

Dominic beamed. "Good. And? Are you going to tell us anything else?"

"I'm staying away from him. I don't want to, but I need to put all my focus on stopping the people threatening the council and the assassins."

"You're already doing that, Win. I don't see how having a boyfriend would change it."

Win sighed. If he wanted Dominic and Kameron to understand what he was going through, he needed to tell them the entire truth, not just a tiny bit of it. "You know Graham, the cook?"

"Of course we do. Is he doing all right?"

"Yeah. He's also my mate."

There was a moment of silence. Win wasn't sure what to expect. He'd never had this kind of conversation with anyone. He knew it was a good thing, of course, but most people would push him to say *fuck it* to caution and at least talk to Graham. Win knew that was the one thing he should do. He *had* to do it if he didn't want to risk losing Graham, and he knew his mate enough that he thought Graham would probably understand why they couldn't be together right away.

"That's great, Win," Dominic said.

Win was relieved he wasn't congratulating him. It was what he'd expected, and he wasn't sure there was much to congratulate him over right now.

"It is," Kameron agreed. "Although you don't look that happy about it."

"I *am* happy. I just don't know what to do about it. I don't want to start anything now, not when I have to focus on keeping people alive. Being with Graham would be a distraction, and I can't afford that."

"Have you ever thought that maybe you *need* a distraction?"

"No."

"You work too hard, Win. I understand why, of course, and I'm grateful you care so much about this, but you're not going to get better results by exhausting yourself and thinking about this twenty-four seven. We all need something warm to welcome us when we're done with the direness of the job. You have to take a step back sometimes, and what would be better to do that than to go back to your mate and spend some time with him?"

Win understood what Kameron was saying, but he wasn't sure he shared that opinion. He'd always done fine without anyone waiting at home for him. Kameron and Dominic were used to having their mates by their side, so they probably didn't remember what their life was like before.

He didn't tell them that. He promised them he'd think about it, and when the three of them left the bar where they'd eaten, he hovered behind. He wanted to go home to Graham, but talking to Kameron and Dominic had made him realize just how much Graham did for him, and how much it meant to him. He wanted to do something for Graham, to show him how much he appreciated everything, even though he'd never said it and he didn't show it.

What should he do, though? He checked the phone, grimacing at how late it was. He'd wasted too much time today, but he supposed he could waste another half hour. Like Graham had told him, his files would still be there when he'd get home.

Graham put the leftovers into the fridge. He'd kept the plate he'd made for Win in the microwave, though. Even if Win didn't want to eat when he came back, Graham would make sure he did. He was used to fighting this out by now.

Once Graham was done cleaning up, he grabbed the plate and went downstairs, hoping Win would be back. He was worried. Win didn't usually spend time out of the warehouse, not this much anyway. He went out often to meet with the council, but it had been hours, and the council meetings always broke up before lunch. And why hadn't he called once he'd realized he'd be late? He didn't owe anything to Graham, but Graham would have appreciated it. He realized he was the only one worrying the way he was, though. Everyone else seemed to think Win was merely doing his job, and while Graham knew he was, he didn't think it was fair for him to do so much. He barely had any free time. It was what he wanted, but that didn't make it fair or sustainable.

He smiled when he saw the light on in Win's office. The door wasn't all the way closed, and he peeked inside, quickly knocking on the door frame. "Win?"

There was a pause before Win said, "Come in, Graham."

Graham was surprised at how agreeable Win sounded, but he didn't ask him to repeat himself. He pushed the door open and plastered a smile on his face. He knew Win wouldn't stay that way when he'd realize Graham had brought him food. "You're back late," he pointed out as if Win didn't already know it.

Win was standing in front of his desk, leaning back against it. He rubbed the back of his neck. "I know, sorry. Kameron and Dominic dragged me to lunch with them." His gaze fell to the plate in Graham's hand. "I'm sorry. I should have let you know."

"You should have, but you can always eat this tonight, or whenever you're hungry." Graham knew he'd probably forget about it as soon as he started working again, but it was worth a try, and he'd be there to remind him anyway.

He went to the small fridge and put the plate inside. He didn't miss the way Win seemed to move along with him, always blocking the sight of his desk. Graham frowned, wondering why. What was he hiding? It had to be food. That was the only thing they ever talked about, along with Win not sleeping enough and not taking care of himself. "What's wrong?"

Win's cheeks flushed. "Nothing."

"You're hiding something from me."

"Ah, well, not really. I just—this is stupid, but I was in town, and I saw something . . ." Win huffed and stepped aside. He grabbed a bag from his desk and held it out. "I saw this and thought of you. I know I've been a pain in the ass lately, or since you've arrived here, really, and I'm sorry. I'm stressed about everything that's happening, and I feel I'm not doing enough. I guess this is a little something to apologize for the way I've been treating you. I know I'm not the easiest guy to take care of, and you've been trying hard."

Graham blinked. "It's a present? For me?"

"Not a present, not really. Just a little something. As a thank you, you know?"

Graham felt as flustered as Win looked. He hadn't expected this. Hell, he hadn't expected anything different from what he already had with Win—him pushing Win to take better care of himself, Win pushing back and telling Graham to fuck off, albeit not in those words.

He took the bag from Win. "Thank you. You didn't have to do this, though. I'm not taking care of you for payment or whatever."

"I know, and this isn't payment. It's just a thing to thank

you. That's all. I mean, we both know you're going to continue bugging me to eat and sleep, and that I'll be as bitchy about it as I've been until now. I guess I'm trying to bribe you into continuing. I know it's not easy, that *I'm* not easy."

That was the most words Graham had ever heard Win say. He was sure Win talked enough when he was in meetings, but usually the only thing he did with Graham was grumbling and bitching. "What happened?" Graham asked, because something had to have happened. He didn't understand why Win had done a one-eighty when it came to him—to them.

Win huffed. "Nothing happened."

"You're being weird."

"Come on, Graham. Don't make this harder than it already is. I was trying to do something nice, but I can take that back if you don't want it." He reached for the bag in Graham's hand, but Graham pulled back before he could touch it.

"I'm keeping this."

Win rolled his eyes. "That's the reason I bought it, Graham. So you could have it and keep it."

Graham peeked into the bag. He wasn't sure what he'd expected. He might be half in love with Win, but they didn't know each other well. Oh, he knew Win loved his family and cared for them so much that he was ready to put his health in jeopardy for it, that he was quiet and that he liked spending time on his own, that he'd do pretty much anything for the people he cared for. That didn't tell him what Win's favorite color was, though, or what his favorite meal was. He'd tried to find out, but Win never wanted to talk about personal stuff. He barely tolerated Graham berating him for not taking care of himself. And Graham hadn't told him much about himself because Win hadn't asked and hadn't seemed interested in general.

But clearly, Win had observed him. Graham hadn't even noticed. What was in the bag told him that, though. He wasn't sure when Win had noticed he was a huge mystery fan, but he'd gotten him an old, well-thumbed edition of an Agatha Christie mystery. Graham wondered if it was a first edition for a moment but realized it wasn't when he took it out of the bag. That didn't matter, though. Graham had been collecting these books from this particular publisher, and he was only missing a few. He wanted the whole series, of course, but they weren't easy to find.

Win had somehow managed that.

Graham looked up. "How did you know?"

Win shrugged. He wasn't looking at Graham, and he seemed almost embarrassed at the fact that he'd bought the book. "I heard you complain to Milo a while ago. You couldn't find all the books from this particular publisher, right? And you didn't want to buy another edition because the size and the covers would be different."

Graham *had* complained to Milo about that, but it had been a few months ago. How could Win remember that? "Thank you. I—you didn't have to, and I love it."

Win finally smiled. "Good." He shuffled and pressed his hand against his thigh. Graham knew that was a sign that his leg hurt, so he probably wanted some time on his own, hopefully to rest.

Graham doubted he would, though. He'd just come back from a meeting, so he was no doubt going to dive back onto the files he obsessively went over again and again. And of course, Heloise had come back from her job, so she'd have to write her report and hand it over for Win to read. Graham knew Beck was already working on the dead man's phone and computer, but he hadn't asked for details. It wasn't his business. He was the cook, and he didn't want details about what was happening. He knew what the assassins did, and he didn't have a problem with it. They did what the law couldn't and protected people.

And Graham didn't want to know any more than that. He didn't need to. He loved the people he lived with, and nothing was going to change that. "You have to get back to work?" he asked.

Win raked a hand through his hair. "Yeah. I wasted too much time going out for lunch."

At least someone had made sure he'd eaten, and even though he and the other two had probably talked about work, he hadn't been closed in his office, and he hadn't been on his own. "I'll go, then." Graham held the book against his chest. "Thank you, Win."

Win knew him better than he'd thought, or at least than Win had let show. Maybe Graham did have a chance to get through to him after all.

CHAPTER THREE

Win had had enough of meetings. He wanted a week-long vacation. No, wait. A *month*-long vacation. He didn't want to have to think about anyone's safety, about marks and who he was going to send out. He didn't want to think about his job and what the fuck was happening, whether someone was going to get hurt. He just wanted to sleep for a week, eat as much as he could, and possibly, cuddle up with Graham.

Of course, he'd actually have to tell Graham they were mates if he wanted that. It wasn't time yet, though. Things were getting messier with every person the assassins took out. The rest of the group had realized what was happening by now, and only a few outsiders had tried killing the assassins since then. Win wasn't surprised—by now, they had a reputation. They'd successfully gotten rid of the first assassins that came after them, they were killing off the members of the anti-council group one by one, and they were all alive and well. They were a force to reckon with, and everyone knew it now, which was why the remaining members of the anti-council group were freaking out.

They were disappearing from the public eye, but that didn't mean the assassins couldn't find them.

Win waited until everyone was sitting to start talking. "All right, people. Quiet down. I have three new assignments." The council had contacted them after Armand had finally come back from his last assignment. There were only a few members left in that anti-council group, and they were frightened.

That wouldn't stop the assassins from finding them and getting the answers they needed.

"Who are you choosing this time around?" Miles asked.

Win scowled at him. "Shut up. And you." He picked one of the three files on the table and pushed it toward Miles. "You know the deal. Ulric, you have the second one. Evan, the last one." He handed them the files and leaned back in his chair. "Same thing as before. Find them, get all the info you can from them, kill them, and bring back their phones and computers. The sooner you manage that, the better it will be, but don't rush."

Miles grinned cheekily. "I'll be the first one back."

Win rolled his eyes. "As long as you do the job correctly, I don't care." He knew Miles would do what he had to do, though. He might be a goofy know-it-all, but he knew what he was doing when it came to the job. "Let me know when you're leaving, the three of you. I don't have anything else to say, so you can all go."

There were a few grumbles from the ones who hadn't been selected, but this was something Win cared about. He wanted all his assassins to be there for the meeting unless they were out on a job. This was something they were doing together, and they had to work like a unit, not like individuals.

The room cleared, but when Win looked up, he noticed Evan was still sitting on the other side of the table. He'd opened the file, and he was staring down at it, his face so pale Win thought he wasn't feeling well. "Evan? I can give this to someone else if you need rest or whatever."

Evan shook his head. "It's not that. It's just . . . I told you about my past, right?"

"I know your father sold you to a lab when you were a kid." Evan hadn't gone deeper into details, and Win hadn't asked for them. Unfortunately, Evan's story was all too common, especially in their group.

"That's about it. The guy who sold me was my stepfather, but he's the only father I've ever known, so I guess it doesn't matter. He's human, though. He's not my mother's mate, and I never understood why she chose to marry him. Not that I care, but, well. Anyway, my stepfather?" He turned the file toward Win and pushed it. "This is him."

Win blinked. "What?"

"The man you want me to kill is my stepfather, the man who sold me when I was eight. And I'll go kill him if you really want me to, but I think there's more to this. I didn't know he was a part of that group, or I'd have told you about this before."

Win took the file and quickly went over it again. There was no mention of the guy being related to Evan. "We only found out about him recently. His name was in one of the computer's we got from the last three jobs." *Shit.* This wasn't good. "I don't expect you to kill him, though. I do think we need to talk about it."

"Probably. Like I said, I'm sure there's something more behind this. He's an asshole, but he's not stupid."

Win rubbed his face. "All right." He texted Beck to join them ASAP. "I'm sorry about this, Evan. I can't imagine how you're feeling right now."

"Don't. I don't care about the asshole. I'd gladly kill him, but I want to make sure we're all on the same page first." He paused. "But I shouldn't go alone if you decide to send me still. I don't know how I'd react if I saw my mom there."

He'd never told Win what kind of involvement his mother had in the story, and now wasn't the moment to ask. Win didn't think it mattered anyway. "I won't send you. I'm not going to do that to you, no matter how you felt about the man. It wouldn't be fair, and to be honest, I don't want to risk it. There's no way to know how you'll react at seeing him again after what he did to you. I can't risk it."

Evan nodded tightly. "I understand."

"Good. Thank you."

Beck walked in, a frown on his face. "Win? Is there a problem?"

"Not a problem, exactly, but I handed the Moore file to Evan, and it turns out that Reginald Moore is Evan's stepfather."

Beck paled. "What? All the research I did said he doesn't have children."

"I know. I'm not saying you made a mistake."

"I never took his name, or my mother's," Evan offered. "Besides, I doubt you'd have thought about pulling my file up next to his. It's okay, Beck."

"I'm so sorry."

"Like Evan said, it's okay. He doesn't blame you, and neither do I. And I know the file is as precise as possible, considering your means. But Evan thinks there's more to this than what we think."

Beck flopped into a chair. "How? What?"

Evan leaned forward. "I know Reginald. I haven't seen him since I was a kid, but I've always hated him, and I spent the years living with him observing him and avoiding him. He's human, and as far as I know, he doesn't have any kind of contact with shifters outside my mom."

"Isn't that kind of the point? That anti-council group wants the council to die out so they can return to doing whatever they want to shifters."

"Yes, but Reginald doesn't care about anything unless there's money to be made, and that Tiger guy was a shifter. Shifters *are* involved, but they're not the only ones. Humans are, too, and I don't get how they can work together, not when they hate each other." Evan raked a hand through his hair. "This is a mess."

Beck tapped his fingertips on the table. "Well, as far as I was able to find out, the main reason all those people are involved *is* money. The shifters want the council gone so they can deal drugs without being arrested and jailed. The humans want the council gone so they can profit off shifters again. I'm still digging into that last part because how they're going to do that isn't clear, though. Maybe your stepfather knows. He's one of the last, so if he doesn't . . ."

Win had a headache, and this new mess didn't help. "All right. Evan, the mission is on hold right now, but even once it's back on, you won't be the one going. Beck, I need you to dig as deep as you can. Focus on Moore. I talked to the council, and they okayed me bringing in someone else. I'll try to be as fast as possible." He got up, wincing at the pain in his thigh. He needed to do his stretches, and he hadn't been. He was too busy. "I'm going to my office. I need to call the council and make them aware of this." He wasn't looking forward to it. Most of the council members wouldn't see it as a failure, but others would, and the clamors for his head would grow louder.

Graham gently stroked the cover of the book Win had bought him. It was in good shape, especially considering how old and used it was, and he intended to read it.

"That's a book," Armand said. He was sitting in one of the armchairs, his long legs hanging over one armrest.

Graham rolled his eyes. "Wow, Armand. I didn't realize you know what books were."

Armand tried to kick Graham, but he was too far away. "If you hadn't noticed, there's an entire side of the room on your left covered with books. I was just wondering why you were stroking it as if it were your boyfriend's—"

"Don't say it."

"Why is everyone so prudish? I mean, c—"

"Nope."

Armand laughed. "Fine, whatever. So, what's so special about that book?"

"It's old. That's all." And Win had bought it for Graham, but Graham wasn't about to tell Armand that. It wasn't anyone's business, just like the fact that even looking at it made Graham feel all warm inside—and not in a sexual way, which was where Armand's mind would go right away.

"And you like old books? Why?"

"Well, this one reminds me of my dad. He had most of the books in his collection, and they were some of the first I read when I was a kid. He gave all of them to me when I moved out."

Armand peered at the cover. "The ABC Murders. You read that as a kid?"

"Yep. They're not violent or anything." *Much.*

"Well, shit. And here I was worried about telling Payne about sex."

Graham grimaced. "Don't. I'm pretty sure he knows everything there is to know about sex."

The door to the stairs flung open before Armand could go down that path. Graham could tell he wanted to ask more questions, and Graham didn't want to talk to him about sex. He liked Armand, but Armand didn't know what privacy was, and he always asked whatever questions he thought of, no matter what they were about. If Graham let him, he'd end up telling him about the first time he'd used a dildo, and that wasn't a good memory at *all*.

Win strode in, followed by Evan. Graham straightened and smiled at Win as he passed by the couch on his way to the stairs, but Win didn't even look at him. He started climbing the stairs, heavily leaning on the railing. Graham blinked. Even when they bickered, Win always at least looked at him, smiled at him. Whatever had happened had to be bad.

Graham wasn't offended by the lack of indication that Win had seen him. He knew there had been a meeting, but he'd thought it had been over for a while since Armand was in the living room dicking around. Maybe Win had gotten a phone call after the meeting. It would make sense.

"What happened?" he asked Evan.

Evan wasn't a talker, but he'd been opening up a bit since he and Gregory had mated. He was still the quiet one of their bunch, but now, he didn't hesitate to slump onto the couch next to Graham. "He handed me one of the jobs."

"We already knew that," Armand pointed out. "Why was it a problem?"

"Because the man I was supposed to kill is my stepfather."

Shit. Okay, Graham understood why Win was freaking out. "I'm sorry," he said quietly.

Evan shrugged. "Don't be. Reginald is an asshole. He sold me to the labs when I was a kid. I hate him, and I'd happily do the job, but Win won't let me."

Graham thought that was a smart decision, but then, he'd never been in Evan's place. He'd had a normal, boring childhood—his parents loved him and had accepted that he was gay without batting an eyelash, his siblings had tortured him accordingly, but they had a great relationship now that they were adults. Graham couldn't wait to go spend two weeks with them, even though it would mean leaving Win behind.

"What's he gonna do?" Armand asked.

Evan sighed. "He's about to meet the council again since they need to talk about this, and he asked Beck to dig deeper."

Armand jumped off the armchair. "I bet he's blaming himself for not realizing that guy was your stepfather."

"Pretty much. I lost count of how many times he apologized. He's in his office, by the way."

"I know. He's going to try to kick me out because he has to work." That didn't stop Armand from leaving the living room, though.

Graham knew he was going to his mate. Anyone would, and he didn't want to think about how much he wanted to go to Win and comfort him. He knew better. Win wouldn't accept that comfort, not right now. He had things to do, a meeting to go to, and he'd be annoyed.

Besides, they weren't mates, were they? How was Graham supposed to find that out on his own?

"Is there a way for humans to know if they're someone's mate?" he asked before he could think better of it. At least Armand had left, or he'd have teased Graham to death.

Evan blinked. "What?"

"Sorry, I know it's coming out of nowhere. I was just wondering if humans could somehow know if they're someone's mate once they'd met them."

Evan didn't ask why Graham wanted to know, and Graham suspected it was because he knew. Neither of them could be certain, but Graham wasn't stupid, and the assassins weren't blind. They had to wonder why Graham was so keen on mothering Win, and honestly, Graham wondered about that, too. He wasn't usually such a mother hen. He cared about his friends, and he made sure they ate mostly because he was the cook, but he'd never gone as far as he'd gone with Win with any of them. He certainly had never helped any of them to strip so they could sleep more comfortably. Hell, he'd once let his brother go to bed drunk wearing his shoes.

"I don't know of any way for humans to be *sure* of it, but

there are indications," Evan answered.

Graham sighed. He'd known he wouldn't get a different answer, but he'd hoped. "I know. Humans feel the bond even though they don't know what it is and not as strongly as shifters. That means they tend to be drawn to their mate, to want to take care of them and spend time with them. But come on. All of that applies to being in love, too. I mean, I'd feel drawn to a guy I like, and I'd want to take care of him."

"I don't know what to tell you, Graham. If someone asked me how they could be sure they're a shifter's mate, I'd suggest they talk to him or her. It's the easiest way, and the only way to be one hundred percent sure."

"What if the shifter doesn't want the human and lies?" Because that was a concrete possibility. If Graham was Win's mate, why hadn't he told him? Graham could only think of one good reason, and it was that he didn't want him. Not telling him was the surest way to make sure Graham wouldn't push, even if he propositioned Win and Win said no.

Except Win clearly didn't know Graham that well.

If he thought Graham would be discouraged by that, he'd gotten it wrong. Graham hadn't been dreaming about finding his mate, but that didn't mean he'd give his mate up if he found him. He couldn't be sure Win was his mate, but he damn well suspected it, and he knew he wasn't the only one. Graham wasn't going to give up until he got an answer from Win. He didn't care if that answer hurt him, although he hoped it wouldn't. But he wanted to know what was happening, even if it meant hearing from Win's lips that he didn't want him.

Graham doubted that was going to be the case, though. Win would have made it clear if he wanted Graham to leave him alone, but instead, he let him take care of him. He might bitch and grumble through it, but he hadn't pushed Graham away the other day when Graham had helped him take his jeans off, and Graham knew Win wouldn't have let anyone else get so close.

No, it had to mean something, and Graham thought he knew what it was. He was going to have to talk to Win to be sure, but that wasn't a hardship.

He just needed to find the right moment.

"I'm not saying I'm not happy about seeing you again this soon, but I could have done without it," Nysys said as he walked in. He poured himself into the chair closest to the door, his legs stretched out in front of him, a stubborn expression on his face. He crossed his arms over his chest in what looked like a dare to someone to bug him.

Win wasn't going to go anywhere near him.

Dominic cleared his throat. "Since everyone who could come here with such short notice is here, Win, why don't you tell us what's going on?"

Win looked around the table. They were the usual suspects—Kameron, Dominic, Nysys, Quincy, Cole, and this time around, Neil, an elk alpha, too.

He cleared his throat. The sooner he got this out, the sooner they could all go home. "When I went back to the warehouse earlier, I handed over the assignments like we'd decided together. Two of the assassins didn't have a problem with it, but the file I gave Evan was his stepfather's."

"I take it you didn't know about that?" Kameron asked.

"No. Beck dug as deep as he could into Reginald Moore's life, but he didn't find mention of Evan. Of course, that could be because the man is his stepfather and not his father and because he was the one who sold him to the labs when he was a child. I doubt Moore would have wanted anything to remind him of Evan once he got rid of him, so it makes sense that he erased him from his life."

"What about Evan's mother?"

"I don't know. She's still alive, since Moore has been married to her for close to sixteen years. They live in the same house, and from what Beck could find, which isn't a lot, she doesn't participate in her husband's dealings. She also barely leaves the house."

"Is she a prisoner?"

"Possibly. I asked Beck to look into it again, especially after Evan suggested it. He thinks there's more behind this than what we know."

"What more could there be?" Nysys leaned forward. "They're trying to kill the assassins and us council members so they can have free play with shifters."

"I know."

"That's why this group aligned itself with the Beasts, isn't it? The Beasts want us out so they can deal their fucking drugs even more easily."

"That's true, but we're still not sure what the humans get out of this."

"Money. I'm sure the Beasts will give them a part of the earnings."

"Yes, but Evan thinks there's more. He admits that his stepfather would probably do pretty much anything for money, and since he knows Moore and I don't, I'm inclined to agree with him."

Nysys huffed. "I want to get rid of those assholes. I *hate* being a target. It freaks Morin out, and he won't let me out of the house, even though we were planning a vacation."

"I understand that, but it won't do us any good if we ignore the possibility. Because if there is something more to it, more people behind it, they'll withdraw and wait for the right moment for them to strike."

"We have to get Moore alive and interrogate him," Neil

said.

"I agree, and that's what I'm planning to do. I just want to be sure we know everything we can find out about Moore, his wife, the house he lives in, and his associates. I thought we already had that information, but Evan is going to work with Beck looking for more." Win frowned. "This is what happens when I give too much work to Beck. He's great at his job, but he's only one man, and since we want this to be over as soon as possible, he has to rush through the checks."

Dominic tapped his fingers on the table. "Ask Beck if he knows someone we can bring in. We'll do the vetting as fast as we can, but I want to know he trusts this person, whoever it is."

"I will."

"Is there anything else?" Neil asked. "Because my mate is about to pop our kid out, and I want to be there when it happens."

Win nodded. He could have simply sent all of them a message or an email, but the council members were clear—they wanted all the information told to them in person. It meant nothing could be intercepted and compromised, but it wasn't great. "I'll contact you again once Beck is done, but knowing him, he'll want at least a few days so he can make sure he didn't miss anything this time."

"Give him two weeks," Kameron declared. "The other two targets are being taken care of, and since we know who Moore is, we can keep an eye on him. I doubt he'll try anything, not with all his other conspirators dead, plus the fact that he's human."

Two weeks sounded like a lot, but Win was glad Beck would have that much time. It meant he'd be able to sleep and eat decently, unlike when he had to rush through his work.

The meeting disbanded. Neil rushed out the door, making

Win wonder if his mate was *actually* about to have the baby right now. Nysys was right behind him, still mumbling about how much of a dick Morin was and the vacation they couldn't go on.

That left Win with Kameron and Dominic again, and it was the last thing Win wanted. "Goodbye," he said, hoping he'd be able to limp his way out before they stopped him.

Of course, he didn't.

"Win, wait," Dominic called out.

Win sighed. "Yes?"

"Have you talked to your mate?"

"Not yet, no. I haven't had the time."

"I see." Dominic looked at Kameron, who nodded.

"See, we think you should take a vacation," Kameron said.

Win blinked. This wasn't going the way he'd expected. "I don't have the time."

"Of course you do. We just gave Beck two weeks to dig into this, and you already sent people out on the other two assignments. Besides, we're curious to see how Roark can work as a handler, and we won't be able to do that if you don't allow him to take the lead."

"I need to stay at the warehouse in case something happens." But he couldn't deny that two weeks of not doing anything sounded damn good.

"You need to get out of that house and live a little. We have everything under control. We'll communicate with Roark every day and make sure things are going well. He'll tell us when the two you sent out come back, and hopefully, Beck will get more information from their phones and computers. There's nothing *you* have to be there for. You're irreplaceable long-term, Win, so to make sure we don't lose you, you need to take a step back and breathe."

Dominic whipped his phone out of his pocket. "I'm texting both Beck and Roark to let them know that you're not allowed in your office for the next two weeks."

"What?" Win cried out. *What the fuck?* He wasn't a child who needed to be pushed around.

Kameron arched a brow at him. "We're your bosses, right?"

"Technically," Win admitted through gritted teeth, because he knew where Kameron was going with that.

"There's no *technically* about it, Win. The council hired you, so yes, we're your bosses. And we're ordering you to take the next two weeks off. It would be great if you actually left the warehouse, but we'll be satisfied to have you out of your office and away from work."

"What am I supposed to do?" Win *needed* to work. That was what he was there for.

"I don't know. Watch TV. Read. Maybe talk to that mate of yours and solve the problems you have with him. But honestly, I'll be happy with anything. And if you need money to pay for a vacation, you just need to ask."

Win's cheeks heated. "I don't need money." And the thought of being away from the warehouse for two whole weeks freaked him out. What if something happened and he wasn't there? What if he was needed?

Kameron sighed and patted Win's shoulder. "I know it can be hard to take a step back, but that's what you have Roark for. Even Dominic and I sometimes take time off and leave the pack and the pride in our beta's hands. Everyone needs time off, but especially you. You have a stressful job, and it's wearing down on you. It's obvious to anyone with eyes. Take some time to relax, Win. Sleep as much as you can, eat the delicious meals your mate prepares, and when you come back, I want you sharp, because we're taking those motherfuckers down, and we need you to do it."

"Well, shit," Beck said.

Armand had dragged him out of his office, and even though he'd brought his laptop with him, at least he wasn't locked up alone downstairs. Graham always liked when people spent time in the living room and the kitchen. He was always there, cooking and prepping stuff, and it made him feel less alone.

"What happened?" Armand asked.

Beck put his phone down. "I just got a text from Dominic Nash."

"Why is he texting you?"

"Me and Roark. And he wants us to know Win has been placed on forced vacation for the next two weeks."

Graham almost dropped his wooden spoon. "What?" he asked.

"That's all the text says. Well, along with not wanting Win to get anywhere near his office until his vacation time is over. Apparently, Roark and I have to make sure Win doesn't try to sneak in." Beck groaned. "How are we supposed to do that? Win doesn't listen to anyone. He doesn't even listen to Rocco, and he's our healer."

"He needs to leave the warehouse," Armand said. "That's the only way he's going to stop working. You know how he is. He won't listen to anyone, and he's going to try to convince you and Roark to let him help, first just a bit, then he'll take over again. This isn't going to work if he stays here, and we all know he *needs* a vacation. He's been looking more and more like a zombie lately."

Graham agreed. He hated that he was about to leave to spend time with his parents. Otherwise, maybe he could have dragged Win somewhere. It would have given them time to talk, and maybe to clarify things between them.

"Yeah, well, we're going to have to drag him out of the

warehouse kicking and screaming if we want to try that," Beck said with a sigh. "I hate this, you know? He always worries about all of us and everything, and I feel we should do more for him."

"Hey, Graham, aren't you about to leave for a vacation?" Armand asked.

Graham smiled without looking at Armand. "I am, and don't worry, I stocked the fridge and the freezers. You won't die. You'll just have to heat the food."

"That's great, but it's not why I was asking."

Graham frowned and turned. "No?"

Armand's smirk told Graham he probably wouldn't like what he was about to hear. "Well, you're leaving the warehouse for two weeks, and Win has to stay away from work for two weeks. You two seem close, or as close as Win lets anyone, anyway. Wait, scratch that. Everyone here knows you're closer to Win than anyone. The only reason I haven't asked you about it is that Beck would kill me. He *threatened* me, you know."

"What are you getting at?" Beck asked.

"Graham could take Win with him."

Graham blinked. That thought hadn't even crossed his mind. "I'm visiting my family."

"So? Win's your friend, right? Would your parents care if you brought a friend home? And hey, maybe you can tell them he's your boyfriend or something. You two are close enough."

"We're not *that* close." But Graham wanted to be, and he knew his mom would see that right away. He didn't care, though. If he could help Win by taking him with him to visit his family, he'd do it, and maybe it would give them the opportunity to get closer.

That was something Graham was definitely on board with.

"Not yet," Armand teased.

Graham rolled his eyes. "I'll talk to Win when he comes back. He's going to say no, though."

"I'm texting Dominic back to tell him about this," Beck said. "He can probably help. And if he can't, Armand and I will make sure Win goes with you. And I'm pretty sure everyone else in the warehouse will help, too. Armand's right— Win looks like he needs to sleep for about a week and eat his weight in food. The only way that's going to happen is if he stays away. And he should be back any second now, so you should probably go to his office. He's going to hide in there until one of us goes to poke him."

Graham looked at the pots on the stove. "I'm cooking, though."

"We just need to stir every so often, right?"

"Yes. It's sauce for the pasta."

"We can do that. Go to him. Talk him into it. I'm pretty sure you're the only one who can."

Graham suspected he was right. He put the spoon down and took his apron off, hanging it on the hook by the door as he headed toward the stairs. He could hear Beck and Armand whispering, and he knew they were talking about him and Win, but that was okay. If Graham got what he wanted, he and Win would be together when they came back to the warehouse.

Win wasn't in his office when Graham got there, so Graham sat in front of his desk and waited. It wasn't long before he heard the door in the hallway open and uneven footsteps come toward the office. He smiled, knowing he had a fight on his hands. He was looking forward to it because Win always looked more alive when they were bickering.

"Graham?" Win asked, stopping before walking into his office.

Graham turned in his seat. "Yep."

"Did something happen?"

"Nope. Well, I guess it depends. I was with Beck when he got the text from Dominic Nash."

Win groaned. "Fuck. So you know."

"And I'm sure everyone else in the house does, too, by now. They're not going to let you take one more step into your office for the next two weeks." Graham got up and strode toward Win. He was still hovering by the door, and Graham took his hand and pushed him out. "I'm not going to, either."

"What are you doing?"

"We're going to your room. You need to pack."

"I know I'm on vacation, but that doesn't mean I have to go anywhere."

"Maybe not, but you're coming with me to visit my family."

"Your family? Graham, that's crazy."

"Maybe, but come on. We both know there's more to our relationship than what we have right now."

Win froze. "What do you mean?"

Graham walked around him and faced him. He didn't release Win's hand, just in case he tried to run, and looked at him. "Come on, Win. I'm not stupid. I'm human, but that doesn't mean I don't feel the bond between us." Graham was sure they were mates. He just needed Win to admit it.

"Graham—"

"Just tell me the truth. Please. I think I deserve it."

Win sighed. "You're right, you do. We *are* mates."

Graham's chest felt tight. He'd known it, but hearing it from Win's lips was different. "Why didn't you tell me?"

"Because everything is a mess. I needed to focus on keeping the assassins safe, and I knew I wouldn't be able to do that if I had you in my life. You're very distracting, Graham.

Even though I kept you at arm's length, I was always watching you. That's one of the reasons I've been spending so much time in my office."

"I'm—okay, I'm not going to yell at you right now because I can see how tired you are. But I *am* going to do that sooner or later. But now, you need to pack enough stuff for the next two weeks."

"Graham, I need to stay here. Even though I'm not allowed to work, I have to be around if something happens. Besides, you can't just force your family to welcome me."

"Trust me, I won't be forcing them."

"I don't know when we'll be able to be together, Graham. This mess isn't over yet, and even without it, we have other things to consider."

Ah. He was trying to get out of being with Graham. Graham wasn't sure why, but he was going to find out. "Like what?"

"It could be dangerous for you to associate with me since I'm one of the targets."

"Maybe, but since I'm already associated with the assassins, I doubt it's going to make a difference. What else?"

"My leg. I can't give you—"

"Stop right there. I don't care about your leg, what kind of shifter you are, what your job is, or any of that stuff. I care about *you*, the you inside, and I like what I know about that man. I want to get to know you better, and that's going to happen at my parents' home, because that's where we're *both* going to spend the next two weeks. I'm not taking no for an answer, so you better go on and pack, because if you don't, I'll do it for you."

And Graham would, too. He'd do just about anything if it meant he could have Win in his life.

CHAPTER FOUR

Win glared at his dresser from his bed. He was *not* going to pack. He wasn't going to go anywhere, with Graham or without him. He didn't care what Graham or anyone else said. He couldn't leave the warehouse, not with everything that was happening.

Miles and Ulric were still out to get the two targets the council had named. Win had to be there when they came back, just like he'd been there for all the other missions.

Although that reminded him that he'd never taken a day off since he'd accepted his job.

He sighed and rolled to his side, squashing his face against his pillow. He had to admit it felt good to be able to stay in bed this morning. He was usually up at first light, earlier in the winter, and in his office by the time everyone else got up. But not today. No, today he hadn't gotten up because someone—he was ready to bet it was Beck—had hacked into his phone to turn his alarms off. Win wasn't angry, though, or at least, not as much as he supposed he should have been. He was on vacation, whether he liked it or not, so he might as well take advantage of it and sleep in.

If only his body wasn't used to waking up at the crack of dawn. He'd been awake for a while, but he knew better than to try sneaking to his office. Everyone in the warehouse was taking his forced vacation seriously, and he'd been caught twice trying to go downstairs last night. He'd been scolded like a child both times, and he'd had to keep his temper at bay. It wouldn't do to snap at people who cared for him for doing what they'd been ordered to do, no matter how little he liked it.

"Win?"

Win pulled his comforter above his head and hoped Graham would take the silence as an answer and leave. He wasn't going anywhere, not even with his mate. He wanted to, because what could be better than spending two weeks with Graham? But staying at Graham's parents' house wasn't Win's ideal vacation. He was sure they were good people, but he didn't know them, and he and Graham were still very much stumbling in the dark when it came to their relationship. They hadn't talked about Win's confession that they were mates yet. Graham had tried, of course, but Win had managed to brush him off. He'd hoped he'd be able to do that until Graham left so he'd have two weeks to think and to decide what he wanted. He'd *prayed* Graham would take his absence this morning as a sign that he was staying at the warehouse.

So why was he at Win's door?

"Win, I'm going to come in if you don't open," Graham warned. Win wasn't sure if he was serious, but since the door was locked, Graham couldn't come in, no matter how hard he tried.

Win felt like a dick about ignoring his mate, but he hadn't expected to confess everything to Graham last night, and he wasn't sure what to do about his confession and the way Graham had reacted. Win had been stunned when Graham hadn't pushed for something, for a conversation or answers.

"Win!"

How long would it take for Graham to get the message and leave Win alone? Win realized he was being childish, but his brain was mush, no doubt because he'd had the first decent night of sleep in forever and it was still trying to re-boot. He could call Graham later, once he was at his parents' house, and apologize.

Win listened, burrowing deeper into his bed when he heard footsteps moving away. Graham was no doubt late or something. He had to go, so he couldn't stay for long. That was what Win had wanted, but it didn't mean he was happy about it.

"You couldn't just open the door, could you?" Graham suddenly asked, way too close to be behind the locked door.

Win jumped and pushed the comforter away. Graham was standing by his bed with his arms crossed over his chest and a stubborn expression on his face. Dasha was next to him, looking sheepish. He grinned at Win and shimmered away before Win could tear him a new one for shimmering inside the warehouse, and to boot, into a private bedroom. "What are you doing inside my bedroom?" Win asked Graham even though he already knew the answer to that.

"You weren't opening the door."

"The fact that it's locked should tell you I didn't want to be disturbed."

"I realize that, but I told my mom we'd be there in the morning, and it's already past nine. Besides, people were starting to worry because you weren't getting up."

Win raked a hand through his hair and winced at the tangled mass. He didn't want Graham to see him like this, but he supposed it was too late. Besides, it wasn't like Graham hadn't seen him half-naked already, and if he hadn't said anything about Win's leg, he probably wouldn't care about his hair. "I can't come with you."

"Why not?" Graham looked around. "Where's your bag? Have you packed? You don't have to take too much stuff. My mom won't mind washing your clothes."

"Are you listening to me, Graham?"

Graham shrugged. "Not really. It's not like I didn't expect you to try to talk me out of it."

"Look, I know you care, but—"

"Yeah, I care, and that's one of the reasons I want you to come. Of course, I also want to show off my mate, but since we haven't talked about it, I haven't told anyone, not even Milo, and let me tell you, he was a pain in the ass last night." He strode to Win's dresser and opened the first drawer, ignoring Win's squawk. "Great. I found your underwear."

"What are you doing?"

Graham threw a pair of boxer briefs at Win's face. "I'm getting you out of bed. I don't care what you want or what you think you want. You're coming with me, and if you don't hurry, I'll have Dasha shimmer us while you're still in your pajamas." His eyes widened. "Or do you sleep in your boxers?" He grabbed the comforter and pulled, revealing that yes, Win slept in his boxers.

Win scrambled to pull the comforter up because wearing only boxer briefs meant that the scar on his thigh was exposed, but Graham didn't even flinch. His gaze roamed over Win's body, and he looked appreciative rather than pitying or disgusted.

Graham shook himself. "Right, we're never going to get out of here if I spend my time ogling you." He turned back to the dresser, opened and closed drawers, and threw a bunch of clothes at Win. "Take those and go shower. Unless you prefer to shower at night? Anyway, go dress. I'll pack your bag."

Win's mind was spinning. He'd known Graham could be forceful—he'd experienced it before—but this took the cake. "Graham—"

Graham twirled around and pointed a finger at Win. "No. I don't care about your reasons. I'm sure you think they're good ones, but they're not. You're on vacation, and you're coming with me. That doesn't mean anything has to happen between us if you don't want it to. I wish we could stay in bed for the next two weeks, because I've been dying to get my hands on you since I got here, but I understand that you're confused. I didn't tell anyone what you admitted last night, and I won't until you're comfortable with it. I won't even push to talk about it if you're not ready. But I'm not leaving you here. You should accept that and hop along, because I wasn't kidding about Dasha shimmering you like you are right now. But don't worry, my mom raised two boys, so she won't care about seeing you half-naked."

Win could have continued to push, but he suspected Graham was just going to bowl him over and go his merry way. It was easier to give in. Besides, it wasn't like Win hated the thought of spending the next two weeks with his mate. If the way Graham was behaving was an indication of their future relationship, though, things were dire for Win. He was used to being the one in command, but it looked like Graham would be the boss of him.

"I want to tell them," Graham said as soon as Dasha had shimmered away from transporting them.

He knew he was lucky he'd managed to get Win out of bed and to his parents' house. He wouldn't have pushed so much if he hadn't been worried for Win, but he was. He suspected Win had planned to spend the next two weeks hiding away in his room, brooding and trying to find a way to wiggle back to his job. And without Graham there, he probably wouldn't have eaten enough. Graham could only imagine what he'd have gone back to, and he didn't like it.

"What do you want to tell them?" Win asked. His voice was steady and cautious, as if Graham hadn't just dragged him to meet his in-laws before said in-laws even knew about him.

"That you're my mate. I know you probably don't want

them to know, since you have no idea what to do with me. I just want them to know I'm happy and that I'll be cared for. I know that's what they worry the most about, especially since I can't tell them where I work and for whom." He sighed. "I just don't understand, I guess." He wanted to, but he couldn't if Win didn't talk to him. That seemed like a mirage at the moment, though.

"You can tell them."

Graham almost dropped his suitcase. "What?" he yelled, turning to face Win and almost falling against him.

Win shrugged.

Graham could see he was freaking out. It was in his gaze.

"I said that you can tell them we're mates—as long as you also make it obvious that we're still working things out."

"Of course I will." Graham had felt pretty dire about the next two weeks, but things were already looking up, and they'd just arrived. If things continued the way they were going, he might even have a bonded mate by the time he went back to the warehouse.

He grabbed his suitcase handle and dragged it toward the front door of the house he'd grown up in, but Win's quiet voice stopped him in his tracks. "I never said I didn't want you."

Graham was afraid to look at Win. "I know."

"I realize you're confused about why I didn't tell you and why I'm still pushing you away."

"You're right, I am, although the short chat we had last night clarified things for the most part. But, Win, I'm not going to push you for something you're not ready for, and that includes talking about us."

"You were pretty pushy this morning."

Graham turned to face Win. "And I don't regret it. You wouldn't be here if I hadn't been, and knowing you, you'd have brooded in your room the entire time I was gone. I'm just trying to help you. I hope I'm not going about it the wrong way."

"I know. And I might bitch, but I'm happy to have you in my life, Graham. I'm not sure where to go from here, but we'll find our path."

That was more than Graham had expected he'd get from Win, especially today. They had two weeks of getting to know each other and falling in love that much deeper. Graham wished he could read the future, because he couldn't wait to see what would happen by the end of those two weeks.

The front door opened, startling him out of staring at Win. He grinned and turned to find his mom waiting for him, a broad smile on her face. "Mom!" God, he'd missed her. He loved his job at the warehouse, but he hated the secrecy and the need to stay away from his family.

Graham dumped his suitcase and bounded up the porch steps. He and his mom wrapped their arms around each other at the same time, holding on as tightly as they could.

"I missed you," his mom murmured.

"I missed you too."

They separated, but Graham didn't let go of his mom. He gestured toward Win. "This is Win, the guy I was telling you about."

Win cleared his throat. "Thank you for letting me stay here, Ma'am." He grabbed Graham's suitcase and tried to climb the stairs holding it and his bag, but Graham could see he was struggling. He berated himself for not thinking about it and stepped forward to help, ignoring Win's glare. "That's my suitcase, not yours. I should be the one to carry it."

"Welcome, Win. And please, call me Olivia," Graham's mom said.

Graham could see she was confused, even though she'd known Win was coming. He supposed he would be, too, if his son told him he was bringing his boss along with him for his two weeks' vacation. Of course, he'd have to have kids for that to happen.

Win and Graham's mom shook hands. She looked at Graham, and he wasn't sure whether to tell her now or wait until the whole family was there. Since Win was involved and Graham knew his family, he decided it would be better to tell them the truth little by little. "So, Mom, about this."

Win looked like he wanted the floor to swallow him, but Graham moved closer to him. He didn't touch him because he wasn't sure how Win would take it.

"What about it?"

"Well, Win isn't just my boss. Actually, he's not really my boss because, well, I can't tell you much, but I work for the shifter council."

"I know that, Graham. Are you going to tell me what's going on, or can we go inside? Your brother and your sister are here."

So Graham had to do this outside. "It's just that I'm Win's mate, Mom. We can go inside now."

She slapped the back of Graham's head. "And you think you can get out of talking to me right now?"

Of course he wouldn't. "We'll talk later? Win and I are mates, but things are kind of a mess at work right now, and we haven't had the time to talk yet, so please, don't push, okay?"

She narrowed her eyes, but she nodded, and Graham breathed more easily. He smiled at her and pulled his suitcase into the house. He grabbed Win's bag as he passed by him and ignored his protests. "I'm going to take this upstairs. That's where my room is."

"Why don't the two of you go? I'll be in the kitchen making sure everyone behaves when you come back," Graham's mom said.

He smiled gratefully at her. She could have made a scene or let the rest of the family dive onto Win, but instead, she was giving them a few moments to relax and maybe talk a few things out. He'd need to find her a nice gift for Mother's Day. "Thanks."

"I put the two of you in your old bedroom, since it's the only one available."

Graham stopped. "I only have one bed."

"I know."

"I told you I was coming with my boss, Mom."

She smirked. "I know that, too, and I'm sure we can find a solution. You can sleep on the couch."

Graham huffed. He should have known. His mom had realized something was up a while ago, hadn't she? She'd always been able to read Graham like an open book, even when they were only talking on the phone. "You're not funny!" he yelled after her.

"Graham?" Win asked quietly.

Graham sighed. "Let's go upstairs. Do you need help with the stairs?"

"Of course not. I climb stairs every day."

Graham knew he did, but he couldn't help the mile-wide streak of protectiveness he felt where Win was concerned. "So, like Mom said, there's only one bedroom available, since the rest of the family is here for the weekend. You could move into my brother's bedroom on Monday unless he's staying longer, or into my sister's, but I'd recommend changing the sheets, because she's here with her husband."

"Can you get to the point?"

Graham sighed. "Yes." He pushed open the door of his bedroom. "The bed is big enough, but we're going to have to share it, and I'm not sure you're comfortable with that. I'll take the couch like my mom suggested if you don't want me here. I'll understand, don't worry. Like I said before, I don't expect—"

"Me to do anything I don't want to do. I know. And I thank you for that, but Graham, who said I didn't want to share a bed with you?"

Win realized he probably shouldn't have said that, but he'd been fighting the attraction for too long. He'd had enough. Seeing how easily Graham's mother had accepted the fact that they were mates was the last nail in the coffin of his resolution to stay away from Graham, and he knew it.

That didn't mean he was going to throw himself into a relationship, but maybe in the next two weeks, he'd be able to find a balance between Graham and the job. It seemed they both wanted to, and if they worked together and talked, maybe they could clear things up.

Graham licked his lips. "Are you saying that you're okay with sharing a bed with me?"

"I don't want you to have to sleep on the couch."

Graham arched a brow. "Then why didn't you offer to sleep there? Come on, Win. You can admit that no matter how hard you're trying to resist, you're attracted to me." He leaned closer. "You want me as much as I want you, don't you?"

Win cleared his throat. "I'm sure the rest of your family is waiting for us."

Graham rolled his eyes. "Fine. We'll talk about this, though." He dumped Win's bag on his bed and left his suitcase next to it. "Ready to face them?"

Win doubted he ever would, but there was no running from it. "What are they going to think? Is your mother going to tell them we're mates?"

"Yeah, she will. She knows I don't want to make a big thing out of it, so she'll warn them to keep their pants on and not freak you out. She doesn't want you to run."

"I doubt anyone would come to pick me up," Win grumbled. Although maybe he could call Nysys. He might come, if anything to annoy Dominic and Kameron.

To his surprise, Graham kissed his cheek. "I'm sure someone would, but please, try. My family is a bit much, but I suspect that's the case for a lot of families. You're used to being with the others, aren't you? And they're kind of your family. I'm sure mine isn't going to change anything."

"What are they going to think of me?" Of Win being Graham's mate. Of him having a limp. Of him being a non-predator shifter. They didn't know that yet, but Win had noticed the wooded area behind the house, and he was planning to spend some time there in his shifted form.

Graham took Win's hand. "They'll like you. And before you can ask, they won't care that you're a guy or a shifter. Hell, Mom is probably over the moon about that part. My brother and I have been through our fair share of breakups, and she always has to pick up the pieces. She'll be happy she won't have to do it again with me."

"What about my leg?"

"You have a limp, Win. That doesn't change who you are or the kind of man you are. They're not assholes. They'll look past that, and honestly, it doesn't matter, either to them or to me. If you think your limp or your scar are going to stop me from wanting to be with you, you're going to be disappointed."

Win kept Graham's words in mind as they went downstairs. Even then, he expected to have to field questions about him and Graham, and his job, and about Graham's.

No one asked about that. They didn't even react to Win's presence except to introduce themselves. But after that, they quickly and smoothly enfolded Win into their family. They were trying hard to make him feel at home, like he belonged, and it made his heart ache.

He'd never had a family. He'd been bred in a private zoo by a man who didn't care that he and the others were half-human and not simply animals. And once that man had had enough, he'd sold Win to a lab. The first family Win ever had was the assassins, and that was one of the reasons he needed to keep them safe.

He was overwhelmed. He swallowed and kept his focus on his plate while the family around him talked and bantered. They left him alone, and he was grateful. He wasn't sure what he would have done if they'd tried to draw him into their conversations.

He ran away as soon as the plates were off the table. He'd been offered free rein of the house and the back yard, including the wooded area, although that one didn't belong to Graham's family. He desperately wanted to shift, but he knew it wasn't the right moment.

Instead, he sat on the short wall that separated the patio area from the yard itself and closed his eyes. He took a deep breath and tried to settle his mind down, but it wasn't easy, not when he was in an unfamiliar place with unfamiliar people. He craved Graham's company, but he needed some time to think.

Win heard the door open behind him. He didn't turn around, thinking it was Graham until Graham's brother Marshall asked, "So, you're my brother's mate, huh?"

Win wasn't sure where he was going with this. "He's my mate, yes."

"I guess that's the correct way to say it, since he's not a shifter. Can I sit?"

"Of course." Win wanted to stay alone, but he wasn't about to ask Marshall to leave.

Marshall settled next to him, far enough away that they didn't touch, not even by mistake. He was giving Win space, thank God. "I knew Graham was hiding something. Well, something more, since he can't talk about his job." Marshall paused. "Is it dangerous?"

"No. He's our cook."

"Then why can't he talk about it?"

"Because he cooks for a group of people no one should know about. Kind of secret agents. The place where we live and their identity have to be preserved, but I promise you, your brother is safe with us." Hell, Graham couldn't be safer anywhere else. Almost everyone in the warehouse was lethal, and they'd give their lives for Graham or any of the other people living there.

"That's good. I guess you made sure of that, since he's your mate and everything."

"I make sure everyone who works for me is safe, always. It doesn't have anything to do with Graham."

"I see. Why didn't he tell us about you sooner? I mean, you make it sound like you live there with him, wherever *there* is, right? So he had to know."

"I do."

"It's weird that he kept this big a secret from us."

Win sighed. He didn't want to do this, dammit. But Marshall was Graham's brother, and he was clearly worried about him. The least Win could do was put his mind at peace. "That's because he wasn't sure. I hadn't confirmed it to him until yesterday."

Marshall arched a brow, but instead of asking one of the questions Win was willing to bet he was dying to ask, he said, "Let me guess—you want to stay away, but he pushed until you gave in."

Win was startled into laughing. "Pretty much. I didn't want to stay away because I don't want him. Things are crazy at work, and dangerous, although not for Graham. But I'm in charge of many people's safety, and I didn't think I could afford that kind of distraction."

"That's pretty much Graham. He's a pushy guy. He means well, but sometimes, you can't help but want to kick his ass, you know? We always fought as kids. I wanted to be alone, and he kept on asking what was wrong or whatever. He hasn't changed."

"He wore me down. I didn't want to come, but he threatened to have me shimmered here in my underwear."

Marshall chuckled. "Yeah, that's Graham, all right. He does it because he cares, you know? He wants everyone to be happy, no matter what it takes. He just takes things a bit too far sometimes."

Maybe that wasn't a bad thing, at least not in Win's case, because he'd realized that until this chat with Marshall, he hadn't thought about his job in a few hours. That was longer than he'd managed in a while, and he owed it to Graham.

The thought that he was neglecting his job made him feel panicky, but it wasn't that hard to push it away, not when he thought about Graham and how happy he was to have Win with him.

Win didn't know what the next two weeks would be like, but maybe they wouldn't be as terrible as he'd thought they would be.

Graham watched his brother and Win talk. He'd have given his right arm to be able to hear what they were saying, but they would notice if he opened the door, and that was the last thing he wanted.

It was weird to see Win in the home where Graham had grown up. He'd sometimes imagined himself there with a significant other, especially after his sister had gotten married and her husband had become part of their family but imagining it and actually doing it was a whole different thing.

"This was a surprise," his mom said.

Graham hadn't heard her, but he was used to being startled. Some of the people he lived with were quieter than death when they moved, and he'd ended up screaming more than once since he'd moved into the warehouse. "I should have told you, but I wasn't sure."

"It's complicated, huh?"

"Isn't everything? But yeah, it is. There's a bit of a mess happening at work, and Win feels he has to be everywhere at once and to take care of everyone. I think that's why he's been pushing me away. He'd been pushing everyone away, to be honest. That's why he hadn't told me I was his mate sooner."

"He's too thin."

Graham smiled. Trust his mom to want to fatten Win up. "I know. I've been doing my best to keep him fed and to make sure he gets enough sleep, but I can't be with him twenty-four seven."

"Or maybe you can now that he's admitted you're his mate."

"Maybe." Graham hoped so. It felt like having Win admitting it was a huge step forward, just like the vacation was, forced or not. They might not lead to anything, but maybe they would. Having Win relax *had* to change something, right?

"Why don't you go join him? Tell Marshall I need his help to clean the kitchen," Graham's mom said.

"He's not gonna be happy."

"And since when do I care?"

Graham laughed. He loved living with the people at the warehouse, but nothing beat being with his family. Of course, he'd be more than ready to run away by the time his two weeks were over, but in the meantime, he was going to soak it all in. "Will do." He kissed his mom's cheek. "Thanks."

She patted his back. "What for?"

"For not saying no when I told you I wanted to bring my boss along."

"Graham, I knew there had to be something more to it. There was no way you'd bring your *boss* along for your vacation if he wasn't more than your boss."

"Technically, he isn't yet."

"Pfft. Like you just said, it's a technicality. There's going to be more, I know it."

"How?"

"The way he looks at you. That man is half in love with you, maybe even more. He might not have admitted it yet, maybe not even to himself, but it's there. Besides, I might not be a shifter, but that doesn't mean I don't know how this works. Love is love, whatever species you belong to."

"So you don't care that I'm going to be with a shifter?" Graham already knew the answer to that but hearing it from his mom would make him feel better. It didn't make sense, but he needed the reassurance.

His mom cuffed him gently on the back of the head. "Of course not. I'm *glad* your future is going to be with a shifter. I won't have to dry your tears because you broke up with your guy again, and I know you'll live a long life with a man who would do anything for you. What more can a mother want?"

That made Graham choke a little. He didn't want to think about losing his parents and his siblings, though, so he smiled at his mom and opened the back door. Both Win and Marshall turned to look at him, and Graham pointed at the door. "Marsh, Mom wants you."

Marshall groaned. "What is it?"

"She said she needs help cleaning the kitchen."

"Again? We cleaned yesterday."

"Yes, again!" Graham's mom yelled from inside. "Move your butt and come here, Marshall!"

Graham pressed his lips together not to laugh, but he didn't manage, especially not when his brother stuck his tongue out at him. Graham knew Marshall didn't mind, though. He patted Graham's shoulder as he passed next to him, and Graham tried to relax. He wasn't sure what he wanted to tell Win. Too many things, that was for sure. But he didn't want Win to feel pressured. He'd promised him not to push, and they had two weeks to smooth things out and decide what their next step would be.

"Hey," he said when he got closer.

Win smiled. He already looked more relaxed, and it made Graham happy. Win didn't have enough good moments in his life, and Graham hoped he'd be able to change that.

"Do you want me to go?" Graham asked.

"No. You can take your brother's place if you want."

"Was he bugging you? Because I apologize if he was." Graham was going to *kill* Marshall if he'd even tried giving Win the I'll-kill-you-if-you-hurt-him speech.

"No, and don't worry. I'm used to handling worse people than him."

That much was true. Win had a strong personality, and he wasn't easily intimidated. He wouldn't have lasted one day at his job otherwise.

Graham settled next to him, closer than Marshall had been, close enough that if they both wanted it, he could lean over and kiss Win. And damn if he didn't want to do just that. "How are you feeling? Still pissed that you were forced to come?"

Win shrugged. "Not pissed, exactly, but I hate not being home. I hate not knowing what's happening and feeling like I can't do anything."

"You take on too much. I know you're the guy in charge, and I can't say I've ever been in that position, but it can't do you good to obsess over everyone's safety every second of every day."

Win sighed. "I know it's not good for me. There's no way to stop it, though. I doubt I'd be able to even if I were fired tomorrow. The assassins, they're my family. We became one little by little, and I don't want any of them to get hurt."

Graham took a chance and reached for Win's hand. When Win didn't move away, he grabbed it and squeezed, not letting go. "I know. It's easy to see how much you care for everyone, and how much they care for you. I'm not trying to change you, Win. I just want a small place in your life." Or a big one, possibly, but Graham would take what Win was ready to give him.

"I'm sorry I've been treating you badly," Win whispered.

Graham didn't want him to be sorry. "I don't care, as long as you know you can't push me away anymore. I wouldn't have let you before, but now that I know I'm your mate, I'm not going anywhere. I won't push you for anything, be it bonding or even only being together, but I'm here to stay, Win." Unless he told Graham that he didn't want him in his life and he meant it, but Graham hoped it wouldn't come to that.

"I just feel like I shouldn't be thinking about you and being happy with you, not when my family is under attack. I *have* to focus on that until it's solved."

Graham had expected that, so he wasn't disappointed by Win's reaction. "Okay, but what about at night when you go to bed? Do you think we could spend time together then, even a few minutes? Because I've been falling in love with you for a while, Win, and I don't want to go back to how we were before."

Win was silent, and Graham could feel him watching him.

He didn't look back, hoping to give Win the time he needed to think over his words and to formulate an answer.

"You're falling in love with me?" Win finally asked.

"Yes. And like I said, I don't mind waiting and giving you time and space. I just want to know I have something to wait for."

"You do. And I'll try harder to give myself time off work."

Graham knew it wasn't going to be easy for Win. He felt like he was in charge of everything, responsible for everyone's safety and happiness. But he wasn't alone—Roark had started working with him, and Win could no doubt give him some of his responsibilities if he wanted to. Maybe being away for two weeks would show him that.

"Can I kiss you?" Graham asked, his voice barely more than a whisper.

Win nodded almost immediately, and the knot in Graham's chest loosened.

He had a chance. Win was opening up to him.

He turned slightly so he could get to Win's lips more easily and cupped Win's cheek with his free hand. Win licked his lips, and Graham couldn't look away. He did so only when he was too close to Win's face to look without going cross-eyed.

He sighed when their lips met. They were both hesitant, moving slowly, but it was everything Graham wanted.

They had time. They had all the time in the world now that Win had finally let him in.

CHAPTER FIVE

Win made his way between the trees, stretching his neck to eat some of the grass on the ground. He was a bit self-conscious, but he knew no one would have anything to say, or at least, that Graham's family wouldn't. He wasn't sure about the neighbors, so he'd made sure not to shift until he was already in the wooded area and as far away as possible from them.

He rubbed his side against a tree. It was soothing, and it took care of an itch. He had to be careful where he stepped, because his bad leg shifted along with him, and the last thing he wanted was to end up face-first on the ground, but the terrain was clean and stable. It wasn't a real forest, but it was enough for him to feel freer than he had in a long time.

It had been too long. He'd been so focused on his work that he'd forgotten about his okapi half. It was always there, of course, but it was so easy to ignore it and stay in human form. It was the form he needed to communicate and to plan, to keep his family safe. His okapi would be no good with that. It was an herbivore, and it wouldn't scare a child. That wouldn't have mattered if Win was an assassin, but he wasn't. He was their handler, and he didn't have special powers like the assassins did. Evan was a chameleon shifter, but he was lethal. Win was just cute.

He huffed at himself and pulled on more grass. He didn't want to eat too much because Graham's mom was a great cook, but he liked the taste of grass, and it appeased his okapi to do something okapi-like, not to have to focus on the human part for a while. Of course, there were other ways to make the okapi happy, but Win was still hesitant about that.

Things between him and Graham were going well. They'd finally talked, something Win had been avoiding for weeks—hell, for months—and Graham hadn't pushed, just like he'd promised. He'd told Win they could take their time and get to know each other, but the thing was that Win already knew Graham. He'd observed him for so long that he knew a lot about his mate.

He knew what spoon Graham preferred when he cooked and which one he used when he baked. He knew Graham wasn't a baker, but he always made sure the assassins had something sweet to eat because he knew some of them had a sweet tooth—Win included, something that was obvious from his appearance.

Win supposed he needed to get over that. He wasn't an assassin, and he'd never be one. He couldn't be, not when he'd walked nearly his entire life with a limp. That meant he was just a normal guy, nothing like the people he lived with. Sometimes he wondered if Graham wouldn't have preferred someone else as his mate, maybe Ulric or Lawrence, or even Frazer, who was human but had the ability to control electricity. Win didn't understand why fate had thought it was a good idea to stick him with Graham, but he wasn't going to complain, not when he was in love with his mate and wanted to spend the rest of his life with him. He'd been lucky, and while they still had to sort things out and solve the problem of the people trying to kill the assassins, the past few days had made Win realize he didn't want to be without Graham.

He wanted to bond with his mate.

Win had wanted that since the first time he'd seen Graham, of course, but when he'd decided to stay away from him to focus on work, he'd done his best not to think about bonding. Now that he and Graham were talking and taking steps forward in their relationship, bonding was very much at the front of Win's mind. The only reason he hadn't asked Graham yet was that he needed to know how things were going at home first. He had to be sure that things were going well, or as well as they could considering there were still people planning to kill them.

Win was in love, and for the first time since he'd realized that, he wanted everything that came along with that feeling. He wanted to spend time with Graham, to talk to him about how their days had gone, to rant about how stupid some of the assassins could be when they weren't out on jobs. He wanted Graham to complain about how much everyone in the house ate. Win loved what they had now, but he knew they could have so much more, and he knew that if they didn't, it was his fault. Maybe this vacation would be the occasion for him to finally let go of the fears and doubts and embrace what he'd been supposed to embrace since day one — his mate and the bond between them.

"Win?"

Win would have smiled if he'd been in his human form. Instead, he looked up, trying to see where Graham was. He wasn't surprised to see his mate hovering in his parents' backyard rather than coming into the trees. Graham was walking on eggshells around Win, probably afraid to startle him into running. That would never happen, but Graham didn't know that, because Win hadn't told him yet.

He would, and soon.

Win wiggled his ears and called out to Graham. Graham jumped back and laughed. "I wasn't expecting that," he said, carefully making his way to where Win stood.

Win wasn't used to having people see him in this form. He didn't shift at home because he was too big to be able to do so without causing damage except maybe in the garage, and who would want to shift in a garage?

"Can I touch you? You can say no if you don't want me to. Although of course, you can't speak right now. You can shake your head, though."

Win didn't smile because he didn't want to freak Graham out. Instead, he moved closer, sniffing Graham's hair and getting a laugh out of him when he tickled his ear.

"I get that you don't mind if I touch you," he said. He looked around and put the bundle of clothes he'd been holding on a low branch before facing Win. He moved slowly, extending his arm toward Win and leaving him the chance to back off.

Win wasn't going to, not anymore.

He pushed his nose against Graham's palm. Graham laughed again and moved closer, rubbing his fingers up Win's nose to the top of his head. Win wiggled his ears, enjoying the smile on Graham's face.

"Okay, so I know you're an okapi. I'm just not sure what an okapi *is*, so don't be offended by my questions, okay?"

Win huffed. Not a lot of people knew what okapi were, so he wasn't surprised.

Graham slid his hand down Win's neck to his leg, fingering the stripes there. "These look like zebra stripes, but you're not a zebra."

Win shook his head. He wanted to shift and explain what he was to Graham, but he enjoyed his mate's hand on his body too much, especially when Graham scratched underneath his jaw. Win closed his eyes and tried to remember the last time someone had petted him this way. He couldn't. He usually shifted alone, and he didn't let anyone close enough to rub him, not even as a human.

"You're gorgeous, you know," Graham said. There was a hint of awe in his voice, and Win believed him.

He'd never thought of himself as gorgeous, not even in

his okapi form, but especially not in his human one. He knew he wasn't — he wasn't tall or muscled, he didn't have a six pack, and of course, there was his leg. The scar on his thigh was obvious in both his forms, and it was ugly. He'd learned to live with it, but that didn't mean he didn't know the reality of it.

But Graham didn't seem to care about any of that. Win wasn't sure what to do about it, how to behave. He was used to thinking about his body as the means to an end, a vessel he needed to do his job. He ignored it the rest of the time because what was he supposed to do with it? It wasn't beautiful or useful.

Graham didn't think so, though. Win would never get rid of the scar, and he'd always limp, but Graham didn't even seem to see that. When he looked at Win, he saw the entirety of him, not just what Win saw.

That was one of the reasons Win loved him.

Graham had never seen an okapi, and he was fascinated. The fact that it was Win, that Win understood everything he was saying and doing, was just as incredible, if not more so.

And Win wasn't running. Graham had half expected him to do just that after they'd talked the day they'd arrived, but he was still there. He hadn't talked about leaving, either. Graham knew he was worried about what was happening back home, but Roark and Beck had told him not to call, and he hadn't so far. He knew they'd contact him if anything happened, and they were only one shimmer away.

"Wanna shift?" Graham asked. He enjoyed spending time with Win the okapi, but he'd prefer Win the human right now. It would be easier to get closer to him that way.

Win nodded with his big head. Graham caught it between his hands and pressed his lips between Win's eyes. Win blinked, and Graham smiled against his soft fur. "I'm going to turn around so you can shift and dress, okay?" Graham didn't want to turn, but he knew Win was self-conscious. He couldn't wait until he could tell Win that was bullshit and that he was the most gorgeous man he'd ever seen — because he was. Graham didn't give a fuck about Win's leg or the fact that he wasn't a super shifter like the assassins were. Actually, he was glad Win would never have to go on missions. He didn't know how Milo dealt with it when North did. How could he not be afraid that North wouldn't come back?

Graham turned around and grabbed the clothes from the branch he'd left them on. He closed his eyes so Win would know he wasn't watching him and held the clothes out to him, twisting his upper body.

Win took the jeans first, then the t-shirt. Graham heard him shift behind him, but he waited until a gentle hand touched the back of his neck. He smiled and leaned into it. "Hey, do you do massages? Because I'd kill for one."

"I thought you'd been relaxing."

"I am. Well, as much as I can relax with Marshall in the house."

Win chuckled and pressed both hands on Graham's shoulders. He dug in, making Graham groan. Graham kept his eyes closed and leaned back. He could feel Win's body behind him, and he wanted to touch him, but he'd make do with the massage, because Win was *good.*

He startled when Win kissed the side of his neck. "All right?" Win asked.

Graham was more than all right. "Yep. You can do it again. Actually, *please* do it again. I beg you."

Win chuckled and obeyed.

It was weird to see him like this. Graham had always known there was a gentle, warm side to him, but he hadn't had the chance to see it before, not when Win spent most of his time hidden away in his office. His job didn't give him a lot of opportunities to smile and have fun, and Graham was seeing a whole new side of him.

He loved it.

And he wanted to push. God, he wanted to push *so much*. He wanted walks in the moonlight, massages, and kisses. He wanted Win to touch him when they were in bed together at night instead of staying so far away that he risked falling off the mattress with every movement he made. He wanted cuddles and popcorn in front of the TV.

And he wanted all that to continue when they went home. He wasn't sure he'd get that, though. Win was more relaxed, and they were making steps forward, but was it enough to make Win realize that having a personal life was as important as his professional one? Graham hated thinking they might go back to what they had before. He didn't want to, but how could he stop it?

"You're not into this, Graham."

Graham blinked. Win wasn't massaging him anymore, and he hadn't even noticed. "Sorry. I was thinking."

Win stepped around Graham to look at him. "About what? Because that looked like some heavy thinking, and you're on vacation. I hope you're not wondering if the people back home are eating enough, because you know they are. It would take more than you leaving for two weeks for them to be underfed, especially with all the food you left them."

"I know. And no, I wasn't thinking about them."

"Ah. You were thinking about us?"

"I was."

Win nodded. "I understand. I spend a lot of time thinking about us, too. We're in limbo, aren't we?"

"Kinda. I love spending more time with you, don't get me wrong. But I hate not knowing what's next. I'm a planner. I have to be, because that's the secret to cooking for so many people. I *hate* not being able to plan, and whatever's between us won't allow me to do that." He smiled. "But I understand it's on me, so don't worry."

"We still have some time here. Can we just take it?"

Graham wanted to say no, but he nodded. He'd promised Win he'd give him all the time he needed, and he was going to do it, no matter how hard it was for him. Besides, it wasn't as hard as Win being away from the people he cared for was, or him not being able to do anything right now. Graham understood why the council had told Win to take a vacation, and he agreed with it, but he also understood how hard it was for him.

He was the guy in charge, except right now, he wasn't in charge. That had to be hell for him, and it added to their uncomfortable situation.

Graham smiled back at Win. "Of course we can. I meant it when I told you I wouldn't push. Do I wish things were different? Yeah, I do. Do I wish you'd just throw whatever doubts you have to the wind? Hell, yes. Sleeping next to you is torture, but I can take it. I can take a hell of a lot of stuff if it means you're happy."

Win licked his lips. "I know you probably think I'm behaving like a prudish virgin."

"No. I don't think that. I think you're behaving like someone who's scared."

Win frowned. "I'm not scared of you."

"Not of me, no. But you're scared because you don't have control over this, not entirely. You're the guy in charge for the rest, right? You're the one who makes sure everyone is safe and stays in one piece. You're the one who hands out jobs and picks who can or cannot move into the warehouse. You're always in control. You have to be. But in this, you can't be because I'm in the middle of it. You can push me away, but you can't control what I'm going to do, how I'm going to react to it."

Win cocked his head. "How do you know that?"

"I've spent a lot of time watching you, Win. I might not have known we were mates, but I knew you were special. I've wanted you for a while, you know."

Win's smile was hesitant, but it was there. "I'm scared."

"I know. I want to tell you that you don't need to be, but I realize it's not that easy. But I'm not in this to hurt you or to change you, Win. I realize that being with you will mean long hours on my own because you have to work. I don't care. I spend a lot of time in the kitchen. I know how this works, and I *like* that you care so much for your friends. I hope you'll find some time for me, but I don't expect you to drop everything for me. I want to be part of your life, but I won't demand to *be* your life. I know it's not realistic."

Win leaned closer. "I don't know what to say."

"Don't say anything. Think about it. Take the time we have left here to relax, rest, and think about what you want from the future. I'm not going anywhere, even if it takes you years to deal with what's happening. I realize there's something more important than our relationship going on right now and that you need to take care of it. I *want* you to take care of it. Milo's my best friend, and he's terrified every time North leaves the warehouse. So do what you have to do, Win. I'm not going anywhere. I'll still be here when you're done. I promise."

That was when Win decided to stop resisting.

He could still feel the instinct to push Graham away so he could focus on taking care of the assassins with one hundred percent of his focus. But he understood what Graham was saying.

Graham knew. He knew how important the assassins—Win's *family*—was, and he cared for them as much as Win did. Win couldn't want anything more from his mate. Graham was perfect.

So why was Win still waiting? He knew what he wanted. He knew what Graham wanted. He knew that what they wanted matched.

And he knew Graham was right. He'd been pushing himself too much. He hadn't been taking care of himself because he'd put everyone else's safety and well-being before his own. It had taken Graham—well, Graham and a two-weeks' vacation—to make him realize that.

He'd collapse if he didn't slow down. Besides, it was almost over, unless they found out there really was something bigger behind this than what they'd thought.

And there probably was. Win had seen too much of the world to doubt that. The anti-council group was just the tip of the iceberg, and no one knew what they were going to find once they waded deeper in the water. That meant Win would probably stress out for months. He'd spend hours and hours at his desk.

But once he was done working, he'd have the choice whether to go back to an empty bed or to go back to Graham.

And he wanted Graham.

Things weren't going to be easy, and Win already knew Graham would have to drag him away from his desk and force-feed him, but Graham knew exactly what waited for him. He'd been doing it ever since he'd moved into the warehouse.

The only thing that was stopping Win was himself, and he was done with that.

He didn't think he was ready to bond, not until things were steadier, not until he knew for sure that Graham would be safe. Or maybe he'd change his mind and decide he wanted it after all. But he could be with Graham, even if they didn't bond right away. He didn't have to continue with his self-imposed isolation. He'd been the assassins' handler for a long time, and while they'd never had to face anything quite like this, Win was good at his job. He wouldn't be their handler if he weren't. So he could do this, and he could give Graham what he wanted, too. He knew he could.

"You're quiet," Graham said as they walked back to the house.

As much as Win wanted to stay in the woods for the rest of the night, quietly talking with Graham, they were there for a reason. Graham needed to spend time with his family. He wouldn't have an opportunity like this again soon. He could leave the warehouse any time he wanted, of course, but Win had tightened things up since they'd found out about the people trying to kill the assassins. That meant everyone had to be careful, especially the humans who lived with them. They were more fragile. They didn't have the defenses the assassins had.

It was still weird for Win to spend time with a family, though. They'd welcomed him as if he belonged there, and he supposed he did, in a way. He still wasn't exactly comfortable, but he knew he'd work his way there if he allowed himself to.

"What did the two of you do this afternoon?" Graham's mom asked when Win and Graham walked into the kitchen through the back door.

"Win shifted," Graham answered.

Win rubbed the back of his head. "Thanks for allowing me to do that. It had been a while."

Graham's mom—Olivia, Win had been told to call her Olivia—smiled. "You can go out there any time you want.

No one else uses that area anyway. The kids used to play there before, but they're all grown up now." She raised her voice. "And my daughter, the only one of my children who's married, still refuses to give me grandkids."

"I heard you, Mom!" Tina yelled from the living room.

Win found the way the family members related to each other odd, but it made him smile. It was the same way the assassins behaved, and that meant they really were a family. Win had always felt that, but knowing it was different.

He was part of a family. Two, if he counted Graham's. He wasn't sure he was there yet, but he knew he would be one day if he let Graham into his life, and he'd already made the decision to do just that.

"Now that I think about it, you two are working things out," Olivia said.

Win wondered what she was getting at. He let Graham take the lead, though. She was Graham's mom, so he probably knew what she was talking about.

Graham groaned. "Gosh, Mom. No. Please."

"What? I'm just saying, you two are working things out."

"We are, but we're nowhere near the having kids step. I'm not even sure we want to have kids."

Win's brain was frozen. He was pretty sure he couldn't restart it on his own.

Olivia pointed her knife at Graham. "You know the best way to find out if you and Win want kids? Talk about it."

"Mom, we haven't even talked about bonding yet. I told you, we're taking things slow." Graham looked at Win and smiled. "And I like it. We don't have to rush, and no, you wanting grandchildren isn't a good reason."

Olivia huffed, but she was smiling, so Win knew she wasn't angry. "As long as I'm the first one you tell."

Win wasn't sure what to say to that. He wasn't sure how to behave with Graham's family most of the time, and Olivia hadn't made things easier for him. He needed to focus on Graham and on making him happy.

And on making himself happy.

Because that was the center of this situation, wasn't it? Win had kept himself isolated, had focused on work because he didn't think he deserved to be happy. He had to protect his family before he let himself, even though he knew there would always be something new and just as dangerous popping up. If it wasn't people trying to kill them, it would be something else.

And Win would never allow himself to let go. He'd have to force himself, and he didn't know how to do that. But maybe Graham could show him.

"You're still quiet," Graham said. They were helping with clean-up after dinner, and Win knew he was right.

"A lot of things to think about."

"Please tell me you're not thinking about what my mom said. I don't expect you to think about kids, Win. *I* don't even want to think about that yet. It's way too soon, and even if we'd been together for years, I'm not ready for anything that can't walk and feed itself."

Win laughed. "I know. And no, I wasn't thinking about kids. Honestly, I've never thought about having children, not with the job I do."

"I bet you imagined yourself doing that job for the rest of your life."

"I did."

"You can, if that's what you want. I'm not going to stop you from doing anything, although I'd appreciate it if you talked to me about big stuff before you do it. Well, if we're together."

"We are." But Win needed to *show* Graham that.

He knew what to do. He knew what he wanted to do, and

he hoped he wasn't about to be rejected.

They headed upstairs, and Win was nervous. It had been a long time since he'd last had sex, and it had never been with someone he cared about, and who cared about him. He wasn't quite sure what to do about it, but he supposed things would start once he got naked. That meant Graham would have his thigh in full sight, but Win would have to deal with that sooner or later if he wanted things to work with his mate.

He rushed to the bathroom as soon as they got to Graham's bedroom. He realized he probably looked like a loon to Graham, but he needed a few moments to gather his thoughts — and to get himself ready. He wasn't sure what Graham wanted when it came to sex, and he was about to find out. He was always prepared, though, and this wasn't any different.

Win was going to take this head-on, even though he didn't know how it was going to end, and that terrified him more than pretty much anything in the world.

Graham was reading when the bathroom door opened. He didn't look up at first, knowing it was Win, but he could hear Win hesitating, even after he'd closed the bathroom door again.

And when he *did* look up, Graham understood why.

He couldn't look away from Win's naked chest. There was a drop of water on his collarbone, and it shone in the light from the lamp on the nightstand. It was just there, not rolling down, and of course, Graham wanted to lick it. Instead of doing that, he looked away, but things got worse because Win was only wearing a towel.

Graham cleared his throat. "You forgot your clothes in the bedroom?" he asked, looking around for Win's pajamas.

"No."

Graham blinked. "Oh?" What was going on, then? He wanted to believe Win had suddenly decided to sleep naked, although he wasn't sure he'd be able to survive that. It was hard enough as it was to share a bed, to feel Win move in his sleep, to have his scent in Graham's nose the entire night, to watch him when he woke up, all sleepy and with his hair all over the place.

Graham might be dead by tomorrow morning, but what a death it would be.

Win licked his lips and stepped away from the door. He looked like he wasn't quite sure what to do, and Graham didn't know how to help him because he couldn't think about anything that wasn't his mate's naked skin.

There was so much of it, and it was perfect. Pale, since Win didn't take much sun if any at all. There were a few freckles along Win's collarbones. His nipples were tight and hard because of the cool air in the bedroom. He didn't have a six pack, but he looked wonderfully soft and welcoming, and Graham had to look away before he started drooling. He was already hard under the sheets, and he put his book down, hoping it would hide that reaction. Win probably knew it was happening, but Graham didn't want to make him uncomfortable.

"I thought about it," Win said.

It took Graham a second to put his upper brain back into gear. "You've thought about it?"

"Yes."

"Uh, can I ask what you thought about? I'm sorry, but I'm having trouble connecting the dots." And couldn't Win put on some clothes? This was hell—a good kind of hell, but still.

"About us. I don't think we should bond yet. I don't want you to be in danger, and you will be if you bond with me. I don't want you to become a target. But I want more. I want to stop pushing you away and avoiding you. You were right. I was overworking myself and neglecting anything that wasn't work. I know I wouldn't have been able to do it for much longer, and that I'd probably have broken down. You stopped me before I could."

"Dominic Nash and Kameron Rhett did. They're the ones who put you on a forced vacation."

"And I would have stayed at the warehouse if it weren't for you." He took a deep breath. "I needed this. I needed to step away, to relax and to not think about work for a few days. It showed me all the things I'd forgotten about because I was so focused on work."

Graham licked his lips. "Okay. I'm sorry, but I'm not sure I understand what it has to do with you being like this . . ." Graham waved at Win's chest.

Win looked down and shuffled. "Like I said, I'm not sure we should bond."

"Do you want to, though? Because I do. So much. And I know you're afraid I'll be in danger, but honestly, I doubt it would be any different than just having me live at the warehouse. And before you even think about it, I'm not going anywhere."

Win smiled. "I know. And I want to."

"But it's scary." Graham understood that part. He knew some people would think him crazy for wanting to basically get married to Win even though they'd known each other for just a few months.

He didn't care.

Win was his future. Graham had known that since he'd first seen him when he'd arrived at the warehouse. He hadn't known they were mates then, but that hadn't made a difference. *Waiting* wouldn't make a difference. They both knew it, and while Graham understood Win's doubts and fears, he didn't share them.

He put the book on his nightstand and got to his knees. Win was still by the door, but he came closer, until he and Graham were almost chest to chest, so close that Graham could feel Win's breath on his cheek. Their different heights meant that with Graham kneeling on the bed, they were perfectly aligned for a kiss.

Graham leaned forward and brushed their lips together, but didn't deepen the kiss. "So you're saying you want to have sex?" he asked in a murmur.

The flush went from Win's cheeks down to his chest. "Yeah. I know I've been distant even after we arrived here. I needed to think. I want you, though. I've known that since the first time I saw you, even though I didn't show it to you. I'm tired of staying away from you. I'm tired of forcing myself to ignore you."

"Then stop. Bite me, Win. Bond with me. I don't want to be apart anymore."

Win cupped Graham's cheek. "It's a huge step to take, and you'll probably be in danger."

"Like I said, I'm pretty sure I already am. Bonding with you isn't going to change that. It *is* going to change everything else, though, so please, say yes only if you're sure." Graham would hate it if Win had second thoughts once it was done.

Win smiled. "How could I ever not be sure about you, Graham? I always have been. I just had to face the fact that I couldn't be an island anymore . . . not once I met you."

And then, *he* kissed *Graham*.

Graham was usually the one who took the first step. He was the one who held Win's hand, who kissed him after asking him if it was okay with him, so this kiss was important for him. It was one of welcoming and surrendering, and Graham leaned into it. This would be his future from now on. His and Win's.

Graham was still cautious as he wrapped his arms around Win. He slid one hand to the front, hooked his fingers into the towel, and paused. When Win didn't say anything about it, Graham smiled against his mate's lips and let the towel drop to the floor.

Win made a sound, a mix between a moan and a groan, and pushed. Graham toppled backward on the bed, taking Win with him because there was no way he was letting go of him, not now that he had him. "What do you want to do?" he asked.

Win buried his face against Graham's neck. "Do you have lube?" he asked, his voice muffled.

Graham's cock was very much on board with that. "Yeah."

"Where?"

"I put it in the nightstand when we got here."

Win looked up. His cheeks were still red, and his eyes shone. "Really? You were that hopeful?"

"Yeah. I don't think I'll ever not be hopeful when it comes to you, Win. I want everything with you, and while I knew you weren't ready, it pays to be prepared." Graham slid his hands down Win's back and grabbed his ass cheeks. He wasn't sure this was what Win wanted, but he'd be open for just about anything. He hoped Win would, too.

He slipped his finger between Win's ass cheeks, arching a brow when it touched something slick. "What do you have in your bathroom kit, Win?" Graham asked.

Win shook his head. "Shut up."

"It's almost as if you want this to be over soon." Was Graham pushing too much?

Win sighed and sat up. He wrapped his arms around his torso. "It's not that. I'm just not very comfortable with nakedness and sex. It's going to take me some time to not want to hide. I know you don't care, but it's not that easy to actually believe."

Graham rolled them. He didn't want to force Win to do anything or to make him uncomfortable, so he ditched his clothes and buried both of them under the sheets. He hated not seeing Win's body, but he'd have time for that. They were about to bond. They'd have years, decades, to get to know each other's bodies and to be honest, Graham *did* want this to be over soon because it would mean they were bonded once it was.

He made sure to keep his hands away from Win's stomach and his thigh since he knew those were the areas he hated the most. It was going to take time for Win to relax, but Graham didn't mind. He loved his mate, and he'd do anything for him.

He could feel Win was uncomfortable, even without the bond, and he didn't know what to do about it. "Are you sure?" he asked. "Because we can wait, or we can bond without having sex."

"I don't want to wait. I know you like me the way I am."

Graham kissed him. "I *love* you the way you are."

Win blinked. He didn't say anything, but Graham's words seemed to have hit something, because he pulled Graham down to kiss him and opened his legs wider.

Graham's cock was like a heat-seeking missile. It lodged between Win's cheeks, and when Win wiggled his hips, the tip of Graham's cock caught on his hole.

Graham stilled, letting Win take the next step. He had to.

But when Win pushed his hips up and Graham's cock slid inside of him, Graham had his answer.

He drove his dick into his mate and bit Win's neck at the same time. They needed to be silent since they were at Graham's parents' house.

Win whined. "You can't actually bite me," he breathed out.

"I can try."

Win raised a hand. "It'll be easier this way." He bit the inside of his wrist, ignoring Graham's gasp. Then he offered it to Graham, and Graham knew Win wanted him to take the next step.

So he did. He wanted Win, whatever Win thought. Graham grabbed Win's hand with one of his and sucked on the blood that was welling from the wounds. He didn't grimace at the taste, but it was a close call. It was easy to forget it was blood he was drinking when he thought about what it meant, though, and especially once Win sunk his fangs into Graham's neck.

Graham would always bear that scar, the sign that he and Win were one.

And he'd always have the bond that blew his mind apart when it was born. He'd always feel Win inside him. Win would be a part of him until the end of their lives, and that was exactly what Graham had wanted.

And what he'd gotten.

CHAPTER SIX

Win was self-conscious, but it was almost easy to ignore the fact that he and Graham were cuddling on Graham's parents' couch watching a movie, even though said parents were right there with them.

Olivia was somewhere in the house, but Bryce, Graham's dad, Marshall, and Tina, were there. Win wasn't even sure what they were watching, but it didn't matter.

He'd never had this—this *family* thing, not even at the warehouse. It was the first time he'd allowed himself to relax and *be* part of a family. He wasn't thinking about who was on what job, how they could get hurt, who still needed to hand in a report. Of course, the thought of his people back home niggled at his mind like it always did, but he managed to push those thoughts away with a conscious thought

Graham kissed Win's forehead, startling him. "What was that for?" Win asked.

"You looked like you needed it."

"I'm fine."

Graham winked. "Oh, I know you are."

Marshall made a retching sound. "God, you two are disgustingly happy. I hate it."

Graham kicked him. "Only because you're alone. Shut up, Marshall. I've had to go through worse when you were with that blond guy. What was his name? Andy? Andrew? He was all over you *all* the time."

Marshall grimaced. "Please don't talk about him."

"As long as you stop bugging Win and me about doing

97

what every new couple does." Graham stamped a kiss on Win's lips.

Win laughed. God, he couldn't remember ever laughing as much as he had in the past week and a half. He needed to leave his office every once in a while when he and Graham were back home. It would allow him to become closer to the assassins, to the people he considered his family, and he wanted that.

He knew it would make things harder. He loved his people, but keeping his distance helped when someone was wounded or hurt. He wouldn't be able to keep on doing that if he truly let them in, but it didn't feel like a problem, not anymore.

Something vibrated, and it took Win a second to realize it was his phone.

Graham grinned. "You sound happy to see me."

Win rolled his eyes. "Last time I checked, I don't run on batteries." He slipped his phone out of his pocket.

He'd expected this call for a while now. He'd stopped obsessing over it once things between him and Graham had started to move ahead and when he'd started to relax.

But now Kameron was calling him, and that meant his vacation was over. Kameron wouldn't have called otherwise, and Win prayed no one had been hurt as he got up to go answer in the kitchen.

He could feel Graham's worried gaze on his back as he left the living room. Olivia was nowhere to be seen, so Win leaned against the counter and answered. "What happened?"

Kameron laughed, and the knot in Win's chest loosened. It couldn't be as bad as he'd imagined it to be. "Nothing happened, or at least nothing like you imagine. Everyone is fine. But we've made a decision about Evan's stepfather."

"I see. And?"

"We want him to be brought in. I haven't called Beck yet, so I don't know what he found, *if* he found anything more than he already had. Of course we'll let you plan, since you're the one who has every detail and bit of info. I'm just letting you know what the council decided."

"Who's going to interrogate him?"

"Well, not everyone agreed with this, but most of us do, and we want *you* to do it."

Win blinked. "Me?"

"You."

"But I'm not an interrogator. I'm the handler, nothing more."

"And Moore probably knows exactly who you are, yes. Besides, the council wants to stay out of it for now. That might change depending on the kind of answers you get out of the man, but in the meantime, we're taking a step back and letting you take the lead."

Win was used to taking the lead. He did it every day. This felt like it was bigger, though, like he held the future of the assassins and the council in his hands. He realized he was being overly dramatic, though. "I'll do it, of course."

"Good. Do you already know who you'll send to retrieve Moore?"

"Lawrence and Roark, if he agrees. I think he will."

"Probably. He might have retired, but this is hitting close to him and the people he loves. All right. Let me know what happens. I'd appreciate a message when you have Moore, but I know getting answers out of him will take time."

"When do you want this to happen?" Win already knew he wouldn't be able to finish his vacation, not when something this big had come up. He wanted to stay with Graham, but he knew he couldn't, and he hoped Graham would understand.

"As soon as possible. Since you already seem to have a

plan, within the week? If it's possible, of course. You're the one in charge."

"I'll have to talk to Beck and check with him whether he found anything that might change the situation, but it should be, yes."

Kameron sighed. "I'm sorry to interrupt your vacation."

Win smiled. "It's fine. I already benefitted a lot from it."

"You do sound more perky. I expect a full report when we next see each other."

Maybe Win had more friends than he'd realized, because that didn't sound like Kameron was just making sure he was well enough to do his job. "Of course."

Win hung up and sighed. He was looking forward to getting back to work—he liked his job, and he liked being busy—but he hated having to leave this place. It was like a safe haven for him and Graham, a place where they could be without anyone else sticking their noses into their business, and it was easy to be worried about what would happen next, once they were back home.

How would the others react to Win and Graham being bonded? Would they care? Would they think Win should quit his job?

"You're thinking way too hard. That's how I know it wasn't good news," Graham said as he walked in. He glared at the phone still in Win's hand.

Win shrugged. "Not bad news, either. But the council has decided to go forward and bring Evan's father in. I have to go back to the warehouse. I'm sorry."

Graham nodded. "That's what I expected, so I already told my dad, Marshall, and Tina about it. I don't know where my mom is, but we'll tell her once we're packed."

"You don't have to cut your vacation short because of me. I know you're enjoying spending time with your family."

"Yeah, but I know how hard this is for you, and I want to

be there to support you."

"I know you do, but it's just another day at work for me. You should stay."

Graham crossed his arms over his chest. "I'm not going to. Besides, I'm sure my boss won't mind giving me a few days off next month so I can come back. Hell, we'll probably come back together." He stepped closer to Win and wrapped his arms around Win's waist. "Only a few days, and I'm sure that by the time they come around, you'll be more than ready to relax for a bit. You promised you wouldn't work yourself into the ground anymore, and I expect you to keep that promise."

Win smiled back. How could he not? "I'm sure you'll remind me of it if I don't keep it."

"Damn right I will. You need to take better care of yourself, and if you don't, I will. Especially now that I have a good excuse. You won't be able to kick me out of your office or your room now." Graham wiggled his eyebrows. "I doubt you'll *want* to kick me out."

"Never." Win was done fighting this. He'd opened his life and his heart to Graham, and he wasn't going to change that. The past week and a half had been great, but now he wanted to see how he and Graham functioned and worked together when they were back to their normal life.

Graham had expected this to happen ever since he and Win had arrived. He was surprised it hadn't come sooner, to be honest. No matter how much everyone wanted Win to be able to relax and rest, they were always lost when he wasn't around, some more than others. It was surprising that Roark had so far been able to keep everyone under control. Graham supposed he was lucky.

He *was* lucky. He'd never have imagined he'd go back to

the warehouse bonded and even more in love than when he and Win had arrived. He loved everything that had happened, how close they were now, but were things going to change?

Of course they were. Win wouldn't have the time to be with Graham anymore, not as much as when they'd been with Graham's parents. Hell, *Graham* wouldn't have that kind of time, either. He'd have to cook for twenty people again, and that took a *lot* of time and prep.

But the other couples made it work. Roark was almost as busy as Win, as was Noel, who traveled a lot for work, yet they were happy. Beck spent most of his time in his office on his computer and Armand was regularly sent out on missions, yet they were close. Maybe Win would finally give Roark more work and responsibilities. That was why he'd agreed to have Roark work with him, after all, and now he had more to live for than the job. He'd never stop worrying about the assassins who were out on missions, but Graham could live with that, and he was grateful he'd never have to go through what Milo went through every time North was given a job.

"You're worried," Win said.

They were packing their bags, or rather, Win was packing while Graham stared at nothing.

"A bit."

Win nodded. "I understand. But I really think we're at the end of this, or of this part anyway. All the people who put hits on mine and the others' heads have been dealt with, except for Evan's stepfather. I doubt any of the killers they found will want to continue this, even if they've already been paid, and I doubt they were. Everyone has realized we're a force to deal with, and that's good."

That wasn't what Graham had been worried about, but that didn't mean he *wasn't* worried about it. "What about

Evan's stepfather? You said there's probably something bigger behind him, right?"

"Probably. It's just a hunch right now, so I don't have many details, but from what Evan said and the way the group of people was structured, I doubt that's all there is to it. I have no idea what we'll find, though. That's why we need to talk to Moore. He has the answers we need. I know it."

Graham smiled. "And you'll get them out of him. I trust you, Win."

Win checked his watch. "We really need to go. I hate to do this to you, though. Are you sure you don't want to stay?"

"I'm sure." There was no way Graham was letting Win out of his sight, not when he couldn't be sure where they were at. They were bonded, but what did that mean? What would it mean when they got home?

When they'd left, they'd both had their own bedroom. They didn't see each other often since Win spent all his time in his office. But what about now? Did Win want Graham to move into his room?

Those were all questions Graham didn't have an answer to, and he didn't want to demand them from Win. Win was no doubt going to disappear into his office as soon as they got home, and Graham didn't want to push him. It didn't matter that they were bonded—he still didn't expect Win's life to revolve around him. He'd known it wouldn't when he'd fallen in love with Win and when he'd agreed to bond, and that was okay with him.

He and Win finished packing, and Graham looked one last time at his childhood bedroom. He's been happy in this room, and the fact that he and Win had bonded there made it even more special.

"God, I hate that you have to go," Graham's mom said

when they walked to the front door. She was holding bags, and Graham groaned, already knowing what was in them — leftovers.

"Mom, I don't need you to feed me. I'm a cook, remember?"

"I know, but I'm sure you're not going to be up to cooking today, and Win liked my food."

"Of course he did, and I do, too. But there's no need to give me this." She wasn't going to change her mind, though. Graham had gotten his love of cooking from her. They both enjoyed spending time in the kitchen, even though she'd never made a career out of it. That didn't mean she hadn't been prepping all this stuff for days, though.

Graham peeked inside one of the bags and grinned. "I changed my mind. I want all of this."

"What's in it?" Win asked.

"Mom's pecan pie. It's the best pie I've ever had."

"That's why I baked two," Graham's mom said. "You can each have one."

The knock on the front door signaled the end of the vacation. Graham sighed and opened, smiling at Dasha.

"Are you ready?" Dasha asked. He was looking from Win to Graham, his gaze laden with questions. Since Win was going to work as soon as they got home, Graham would have to face the questions. He didn't mind, but how was he supposed to answer them?

He had no idea what to say, and that wouldn't change until he and Win talked. *That* wasn't going to happen anytime soon, of course. God only knew how long Win would be working. But Graham would drag him out for dinner, because he wasn't going to let Win eat at his desk anymore, not when everyone else sat around the dining table.

"When will you two come back?" Graham's mom asked.

Graham hesitated. He wanted to give her an answer, but

he wasn't the one in charge. He'd had to jump through hoops to get these two weeks approved, although that probably had more to do with the fact that the assassins were still in danger when Graham had asked. He knew it wouldn't be easy anyway, though. He couldn't tell his parents where he was or who he lived with beyond what he'd already said.

"Soon, I promise," Win said.

Graham blinked, because he hadn't expected that.

His mom beamed at Win and kissed his cheek. "Good. You're part of the family now, so I expect you to come along with Graham."

"I will."

Graham hadn't seen that coming, either. He'd thought Win was mostly uncomfortable with his family, and he certainly had been in the beginning, but maybe he'd relaxed enough to realize he *was* part of the family now. It had to be weird for him, but Graham was grateful he was able to give his mate that.

Dasha kept eying them as they finally managed to extricate themselves from the arms of the family members. Graham's heart was heavy, but he knew he'd be back — and that this time, he wouldn't be alone.

"What the fuck did you do to him?" Dasha asked in a whisper, leaning close to Graham.

"Nothing."

"But he's smiling. He's relaxed. I expected to find him walking up and down the driveway and yelling at me because I was late. He's wasting *time*. He's never wasted time before. And he *hugged* your mom."

Graham rolled his eyes. "Just leave him alone. This is what we wanted from a vacation, right? For him to relax and let go of the stress. Don't stress him out again before we can even get home."

Dasha raised his hands. "I won't. Whatever you did, it

was magic, and I won't play around with it. Everyone's going to be happy to see how much better he looks. You work miracles, man."

Graham wasn't too sure about that, but he smiled. Miracle or not, he could feel how relaxed Win was, how happy, and he'd be able to feel it for the rest of his life. He'd be able to tell when Win was hurt, when he was uncomfortable, when he needed to take a step back from work and everything else, and he'd make sure he did.

Because that was what their relationship was about. Win worried for everyone else, and Graham worried for him.

And he wouldn't have it any other way.

Win's first instinct was to run to his office as soon as Dasha shimmered them back to the warehouse. In fact, he was already halfway through the door when he remembered he wasn't the same man he'd been before. He never would be again, because he had Graham now.

He turned and, ignoring Dasha, walked back to Graham. He could feel Graham's disappointment, and he hoped it was only because they'd had to leave his family early, not because of what he'd just done. He wanted to give Graham the world, but he could only give himself, and he realized that wasn't a great bargain.

"What's wrong?" Graham asked when Win stopped in front of him.

Win shook his head. He grabbed Graham's t-shirt, pulled him forward, and kissed him. He didn't care that Dasha was there, no doubt staring in astonishment, or that everyone in the warehouse would know about it within ten minutes. He wasn't ashamed of Graham, and he wasn't going to hide the fact that they were mated.

"I'm sorry I have to go," he murmured.

Graham nodded. "I know. I can feel it. And I understand why. So go and save the world. I'll be waiting for you in the kitchen."

Win felt it wasn't enough, but he couldn't afford to stay and convince Graham he wasn't going to hole up in his office again.

He left Graham behind and limped his way to his office, thankful that the room dedicated to shimmering was on the same floor. There was no way he could do the stairs in a rush, not without falling flat on his face.

Beck was already in Win's office when Win arrived, sitting in one of the chairs in front of his desk. He looked up and smiled when Win entered. "Roark will be here soon," he told Win.

Win nodded and went to flop into his chair. He wasn't tired, but he could already imagine what the rest of the day would be like, and he could do without it. "Tell me what we have," he said.

Beck leaned back in his chair. His laptop was on his knees, and his fingers flew on the keyboard. Win was always impressed with that—he'd never gotten much beyond the use-two-fingers-to-type stage. "I started from the beginning since I had the time, and I *did* find something new."

"What is it?"

"Well, Mr. Moore seems to be friends with a certain Gavin White."

"Is that name supposed to tell me something?"

"No. But Gavin White is a government official. Military, although not as a soldier. He's a scientist of some kind."

That wasn't good. "What kind?"

"I don't know. He's in the administrative branch, but a lot of the stuff he works on is top-secret. I could hack this stuff, but you know I'm not allowed to do it."

Because the council tried to work with the human government when they could. It was a pain in the ass, and Win was pretty sure that the opposite never happened. Even with the council, the humans still treated shifters like they were negligible. "What do you *think* is happening?"

"I don't know, but I doubt it's good. I dug into White's life as much as I could. Everything is normal—he's married, has three kids, you get it. But I also noticed he has a lot of contacts with scientists, especially geneticists. All buried, of course. I had to dig deep to find them, and I only found fragments."

Win rubbed his face. "We've already heard this once before."

"Yeah, we did."

The difference was that shifters had been hidden then. Win didn't know if it would make a difference, not if the government claimed that whatever they were doing was on a voluntary basis and that they needed it to protect the country better. "This isn't good. Does the council know about this?"

"Not yet. I knew you were coming back, so I wanted to tell you first."

"Conference call," Roark said as he breezed in. He was talking on his phone, and when Beck set up the conference call, Win found out who was on the other side.

"Already home?" Dominic asked him.

"Kameron called me."

"I wish we could have left you alone for longer."

"You're not the only one."

The other council members joined the call, and Win breathed out. This wasn't the best way to get back into work after more than a week off, but he didn't have a choice. "Beck, tell them what you just told me."

Win's brain was already going a mile a minute. He'd already lived through this, and if someone asked him to guess, he'd say that the human government had probably opened a top-secret program that had to do with shifters. The most obvious reason would be to make super soldiers. It was what Glass had been trying to do two decades ago, and people always wanted to be stronger, faster, better than everyone else. Win doubted they'd had any trouble finding volunteers. That didn't make it legal, though.

"Dammit," Kameron muttered, bringing Win back to the conversation.

"Are you sure about this, Beck?" Dominic asked, all humor gone from his voice.

"Pretty much. It would be better if I could access those top-secret files, though."

"I'll see what I can do. I have a few contacts in the government, and if we have to work with them, they should have to work with us."

Win snorted. "I'm sure they're going to take it well if you tell them that."

Dominic sighed. "I know. But I want to try to do this the right way before we break the law. I want to be able to show that we tried and that we're not the ones in the wrong here. Of course, if they're doing what we think they're doing, that's going to be obvious."

Because experimenting on shifters had been outlawed when shifters' existence had become public. It was one of the conditions the council had demanded, and since the humans didn't have a clue how to deal with the situation back then, they'd agreed. It wouldn't have looked good for them not to, not when a lot of people were discovering that the people they loved, their partner, their friends, their neighbors, were shifters.

"What's next?" Neil asked.

Win looked at Roark. "I'm going to send Lawrence, and Roark if he agrees, to it to pick up Moore. We're shooting in the dark right now, but that might change once we can talk to him."

"I want to be there when you interrogate him," Dominic said.

"Of course. You're all welcome to come." But Win hoped the ones who didn't like him would skip it. He didn't want to be looked at with contempt in his own house, while he was doing his job.

"Roark?" Kameron asked. "You haven't said if you're going yet."

"Of course I am. I might be retired, but that doesn't mean I can't still do my job when I'm needed." Roark sounded slightly offended, and it made Win smile.

"No one said you weren't. When are you planning to go?"

Beck and Roark looked at Win. He looked back at Beck. "Do you have Moore's schedule?"

"He spends most of his nights at home. He does travel for meetings sometimes—he has a company that deals with security issues, offers bodyguards, that kind of thing."

"Mercenaries."

"I guess. Although I can't find anything bad about the company. Moore doesn't own the company alone, and as far as I could find, he doesn't have much to do with the everyday stuff there. He's not the one who hires or even chooses most of the jobs."

"He's home right now? Tonight?"

"He should be. His schedule says he is."

"And we didn't hear that," Dominic said.

Beck gave Win a sheepish smile, but Win couldn't care less that he'd hacked Moore's computer. "Roark, can you go tonight? Or do you need more preparation?"

Roark checked the time. "I'll talk to Lawrence, but I don't think it'll be a problem. It's early enough that we have the time to go over Beck's findings and be ready by the time midnight arrives."

"Good." The sooner they did this, the better it would be for everyone — except Moore.

"What about Evan's mother? She still lives with Moore, right?"

Win looked at Beck, since he was the one who had all the answers. Beck nodded and clicked away on his keyboard. "They're married, and yes, they live together. I can't find much about her. She's a chameleon shifter. She inherited a lot of money, which is probably why Moore married her. I can't find anything about him being abusive, but from what Evan told me, I'm sure he is. That could be the reason Evan's mom barely leaves the house."

"So it's a rescue, too?"

Beck nodded. "It is."

Win sighed. It seemed like the problems weren't over yet.

Graham was elbows-deep in mincemeat and spices when Milo found him in the kitchen. "What are you cooking?" he asked.

"Meatloaf, mashed potatoes, apple pie for dessert."

"Smells good."

"Thanks."

Graham could feel Milo's gaze on him, but he ignored it. He knew Milo would eventually ask. He had no patience.

Sure enough, Graham only had to count to twenty before Milo blurted out, "What happened with Win, then?"

Graham smiled. "Who said anything happened?"

"Oh, come on. You spent the past week and a half with him at your parents' house. I'm surprised he didn't call Dasha to demand to be shimmered home on the second day."

He'd probably been tempted to, at least in the beginning. "Everything was fine."

"Stop fucking around, come on." Milo leaned closer. "I just want to know if the two of you talked."

Graham hadn't told Milo that Win had admitted they were mates the night before they'd left. He hadn't been sure of what it meant, and he'd wanted to talk to Win first. Milo knew he suspected that was the case, though. He wouldn't be surprised.

Graham cleaned his hands and washed them. Then he looked around, and when he was sure no one else would see it, he pulled down the collar of the t-shirt he was wearing, exposing the scar Win had given him.

Milo gasped. "Seriously? When you left, you weren't even sure you were his mate, and you come back one week later mated?"

Graham looked around again. "Don't yell. I don't know if Win wants everyone knowing about this."

Milo frowned. "Why wouldn't he? He bonded with you. That has to mean he's ready for the world to know."

"Yeah, but there's a lot going on, and I don't want people to be distracted."

"They won't be distracted. They'll be happy."

"Milo, please."

Milo raised both hands. "Don't worry, I won't tell anyone. I'm just curious about why you'd think he wants to keep you a secret, and about why *you'd* want that, because we both know it's not your style."

That much was true. Graham wasn't one for secrets, especially not when *he* was supposed to be the secret.

"It's not a secret, but you know how Win is. He's focused on the assassins' safety. Besides, I don't want to announce this before I've had a chance to talk to him."

"You didn't talk while you were away? Because, again, you came back *bonded*."

"Of course we talked, but not about this. I thought we'd

have more time." Graham should have followed his instinct and talked to Win, but he hadn't wanted to push too much, and he'd been so content while they were on vacation that it had felt like he had all the time in the world. He supposed he did since they were bonded, but that didn't help with his current situation.

Milo kissed Graham on the cheek. "I'll stop pushing. I'm happy if you are, Graham, and I'm not sure that's the case. You should be smiling."

"I *am* smiling."

"Not enough."

Graham sighed. "Because I hate the reason we're back early. I'm scared for everyone, you know. My mate might not go out there with them, but that doesn't mean he won't be destroyed if something happens to either of them."

"I know that, and trust me, I'm just as stressed as you about it." He paused. "Want some help? You just need to put this together, right?"

"It's a risk, but I guess you can. You'll be the one to take the blame if one of the meatloaves falls apart, though."

Milo bumped his hip against Graham, and just like that, they were okay again. They worked in silence, and Graham couldn't help but be distracted. He kept looking at the stairway door, waiting for Win to come back. He knew his mate was in a meeting with Beck and Roark, though, and probably had several council members on the phone. The meeting could last for hours, and it probably would, come to think of it.

The door opened as Graham was cutting the meatloaves. He almost lost a finger in his haste to look up and see if it was Win.

It was. Win trudged in, followed by Beck and Roark. Roark made a beeline for Lawrence, who was sprawled on one of the couches waiting for dinner to be served. The open area that held the kitchen, the dining table, and the living room was full of people—Ulric and Frazer were setting the table, Armand and Tony were fighting over the remote control, Miles was cleaning up the stuff Graham didn't need anymore. Graham wasn't sure what Milo, North, Noel, and the others were doing, but it seemed that they were almost all there. He didn't know who was out on a mission and who had decided to eat dinner somewhere else, but if that was the case, it was only a few of them.

It made Graham nervous. What was Win going to do? Graham was surprised he wasn't still in his office. It was a first, and he couldn't help but wonder if it had to do with him or with the vacation. Maybe it was just that he was more relaxed and had decided he wanted to spend more time with his family.

Graham startled when Win came toward him. He'd fully expected his mate to go sit with the others and talk about work. He wouldn't have minded, as long as they spent the rest of the night together. But Win was next to him now, smiling at him and leaning close. Graham blinked, and the next thing he knew, Win was kissing him on the lips. He kept it short, and his cheeks were flushed when he moved away, but he'd done it. He'd kissed Graham in front of everyone, without hesitation.

A wolf whistle made Win jump away. Graham reached for him instinctively to steady him, and Win let him.

"Would you look at that. He has a heart!" Ulric exclaimed.

"Oh, come on. This was obviously coming. Didn't you notice how Graham always took care of Win?" Armand asked.

Tony just held his hand out, and Evan—where had he come from—slapped ten dollars into his palm.

Win groaned and pressed his forehead against Graham's shoulder. "They really hate me, don't they?"

Graham laughed. Most of the worry that had weighed on his mind was gone. Win didn't want to hide their relationship. He didn't want to go back to what they'd had before. Graham hadn't thought it possible, but he'd been afraid anyway. And now he didn't have to be.

He wrapped his arm around Win's shoulders and kissed his temple. "They love you. That's why they're happy."

"Who said anything about happy? *I'll* be happy when I have some of that meatloaf in my stomach," Ulric said.

"And I want answers. I just lost ten dollars," Evan added.

"You should probably tell them what you want them to know," Graham murmured. "They won't stop talking about it otherwise, and by the end of the week, we'll find out that we eloped and that you got me pregnant."

Win chuckled. "Or the other way around." His cheeks flushed. "You don't mind?"

"Of course not. I'm pretty sure they've all known I was in love with you for weeks."

"All right." Win cleared his throat, and for once, it was enough for him to get everyone's attention. "I'll say this once, and I don't want to hear anything about it after this. And please, leave Graham alone. He already has to worry about feeding you lot. Don't give him a reason to poison you, yeah?"

There was a chorus of groans and yesses, and one *I don't care if it's poisoned as long as I get to eat* from Ulric. Win went ahead. "Yes, Graham and I are together. We're mates, actually, and we bonded while we were on vacation. That's all you need to know, so sit your asses down and eat. Ulric, keep those hands away from the meatloaves before Graham uses his knife on you."

There was a chorus of congratulations and exclamations, and Graham felt so much lighter. Not knowing what Win wanted to do was the one thing that had weighed on his mind, but now that was gone, and he could focus on their future. It wasn't going to be easy, not with what was happening around them, not when they had to keep everyone safe.

But they were together, and that wouldn't change. And together, they could face the world and make things right, no matter how long it took them.

CHAPTER SEVEN

Win was tense. There was no way around it, even though he'd spent half the night in his bed wrapped around Graham before he'd had to leave.

He'd asked Graham to move into his room, and Graham had agreed. He'd do it tomorrow, or rather, today since it was the middle of the night. Roark and Lawrence, shimmered by Dasha, had left the warehouse several hours earlier to pick up Moore, Evan's stepfather. They'd brought him to the council jail, because there was no way Win wanted him in the warehouse where his mate was sleeping in their bed. Besides, half the council was present, ready for the interrogation, and so was Win. He knew this was far from over, not even with Moore in custody. They were about to open Pandora's box, and Win had no idea what was going to come out of it. He knew it wouldn't be good, though.

But that was the story of his life and the assassins. Their group had been formed because of this—because even though the humans had agreed to let the council become an official organization that ruled over shifters and cooperated with the humans, everyone knew it wouldn't last long. Humans—people—were too greedy. Win was actually surprised they'd lasted this long before trying to exploit shifters, and he was glad the council and the assassins had found out. They were going to find a way to get the situation diffused. Win didn't know how yet, but that would change once he talked to Moore, hopefully.

"How are you after your vacation?" Kameron asked.

They were watching Moore through one-way glass, waiting for Win to feel it was the right moment to go inside and talk to him.

"Better. I hate this, but I guess I have to thank you for forcing me to take it."

Kameron chuckled. "You hate it, huh?"

"You know what I mean. I didn't want to go, but I can see now that it was for the best."

"You and your mate?"

Win couldn't help but smile. "Bonded."

"That's great. Although I wish we hadn't pulled you away. Maybe you can go on a honeymoon once this is done."

"Maybe." But they both knew it would be a while before that happened.

Win turned his attention back to the glass. Moore still looked like he was relaxed and didn't care, but Win could see through him. Moore was bouncing his knee, and he was sweating even though the room wasn't warm. He also kept licking his lips.

He *was* nervous, and that wasn't going to get better. "I think I should go inside."

Kameron looked at the glass. "He's ready."

"I think so."

"We'll be here."

Win knew that, and it added to his stress, but he straightened his back and set his shoulders.

Then he went to the room and walked in.

Moore's gaze was on him as soon as he did so. "Where am I? You don't have the right to keep me here. I demand to talk to my lawyer," he said.

Win ignored him and sat in front of him. He didn't have anything with him, but he didn't need anything. All the information he *did* need was in the brain of the man in front of him.

"You were arrested," he said.

"Not by humans, and I don't consider your people anything close to human. Besides, you have no authority over me."

Win crossed his arms over his chest. "What about your wife? She's a chameleon shifter, isn't she? So is her son, your stepson."

Moore paled. Win doubted he'd expected to be asked about Evan. It had been years, and the asshole probably hadn't thought twice about Evan since he'd given him to the lab.

"So what? She's my wife. You're not going to talk to her, are you? Because we're married. She can't tell you anything."

"I haven't talked to her. Her son will, though. I'm sure she'll be happy to see him."

"Her son?"

There was fear there now. Win smiled. "Her son. I've known Evan for a while now. He was happy to find out his mother didn't have anything to do with him ending up in the lab."

"Of course she didn't," Moore snapped. "She's an idiot. Why would I want to raise that kid? He wasn't even human. Of course I sold him off."

Sold him. That was new. Evan knew his stepfather had handed him over, but as far as Win was aware, he didn't know about the money exchange. "Didn't you already have enough money? Your wife is rich, isn't she?"

Moore hesitated. Win leaned forward. "I might be able to convince the people in charge to give you a lighter sentence, you know, if you cooperate."

Moore hadn't struck Win as being particularly brave, and it was obvious he was ready to do pretty much anything for himself. Win hoped that meant he wouldn't try to protect whoever was behind this, not when it meant he might get a reduced sentence.

Moore swallowed. "You can do that?"

"I can. Of course, I'm also the one who decides if the info you give me is worth that. You should start talking."

"What do you want to know?"

There it was. "You said you sold Evan?"

"*That's* what you're after? Does he want revenge? Is that why I was brought here?"

"Just talk."

"Yes, I sold him. His mother didn't want to give me money back then. But her son's disappearance broke her."

Win wanted to slug the asshole in the face. He hoped that this would help Evan, though. "Go on."

"That's how I met Gavin White."

Win perked up. He didn't want to show how interested he was in this bit of information, but Moore would probably know anyway. "Who is Gavin White?"

"He was a scientist back then. One of those who worked on your people. I left Evan with him."

"But that's not the last time you saw him, right?"

"No. He's a big shot now. Government. But I'm sure you already know that."

"I do. You stayed in contact with him, then."

"Yes. He asked me if I could bring him other shifters, so that's what I did. He paid well."

"When did it stop?"

Moore leaned back in his chair. "It hasn't."

Win swallowed. "You still sell him shifters?"

"Yes."

"How do you find them?" Because after what he'd told Win, Win doubted he had shifter friends or anything like that.

"The Beasts."

Fuck. "You mean you buy shifters from the Beasts, then sell them to Gavin White, who is a government official?"

"He's in the military. But yes. That's what I mean." Win turned the sheet of paper that had been left on the table toward Moore. "Write it down. Everything."

"You said you'd help me get a reduced sentence."

"I will." They both knew he wouldn't get a lawyer. No one would know what happened to him. He'd been taken by the assassins, not by the enforcers. They only answered to the council. The human government didn't even know about them, and there was a reason for that.

This was the reason. Moore had sold probably dozens of shifters to the labs and the government. Win doubted most of them were alive, and that meant their blood was on Moore's hands. He had to pay, but the most the humans would do was give him a slap on the wrist. He'd trafficked shifters, not humans. They wouldn't care.

Win left the room. He was done with Moore, and if he had his way, he'd never be in the same room as that man again.

"You got what we needed," Dominic said with a nod.

"And I need a shower after that." Win sighed. "It was easier than I thought it would be."

"He's a man who only cares about himself. He wants money, power, and now, a lighter sentence. He probably doesn't realize how bad things are about to turn for him."

Win rubbed his face. "I have to go."

"I get it. Go to your mate. Try to get some sleep. Moore will still be here in the morning. He's not going anywhere."

Graham was in bed when Win got home. It was going on three in the morning, and he did his best not to wake his mate. He took his clothes off and left them on the floor rather than folding them and putting them on the dresser and slid into bed, shivering. Graham turned toward him and sighed as if releasing a tension he'd felt even though he was asleep. He cuddled against Win's side, and even though Win was exhausted, he looked at his mate.

This was his. *Graham* was his, and nothing would change that.

Win had so much more than he'd ever thought he could have. He'd fought it, but now that he'd welcomed Graham into his heart, he was happier than he'd ever been. There was nothing wrong or bad in holding onto that happiness even though times were dire for him, for the assassins, the council, and shifters in general.

They'd make it through. They always did. And Win wouldn't have to do it alone.

YOU MAY ALSO ENJOY THE FOLLOWING FROM EXTASY BOOKS INC:

The Perfect Three
Catherine Lievens

Excerpt

"Will we see each other again?" Lance asked as Monty walked him home. He sounded nervous, and it made Monty smile.

"If you want to. Besides, Hope isn't that big. I'm sure our paths will eventually cross again, even if you decide you don't want anything to do with me."

Lance's head snapped toward Monty. "I won't decide that."

Monty smiled. "I know." They might have just met, but he could tell there was something there, something that could become more. He wasn't going to tell Lance about it, even though he suspected Lance could feel it as much as he did.

Lance stared at Monty for a second, then nodded. "Good. So, are we going to see each other again?"

"Of course. You know where to find me when you have time, don't you? Just come around and ask for me. I'll probably be busy, but we can have a chat." Monty wanted to ask

Lance out on a date, but he didn't want to push, and he realized how complicated it would be to have a relationship with him. He didn't even know if that was something Lance might want, and he wasn't going to ask. Like he'd told Lance, Hope was a small town, so they'd have plenty of opportunities to see each other again soon and hopefully let things happen naturally. They wouldn't have much time, but it was better than ruining everything by rushing into it.

"Well, this is me," Lance said. He shuffled as he stopped in front of the only apartment building in town—if it could even be called that. It was only three floors high and contained six apartments.

"You're staying here?"

"Yes. Frank kept an apartment for me in case I wanted to come around. I haven't taken advantage of it yet, not until now."

"I see. Well, goodnight, Lance." Monty wanted to kiss him goodnight, but again, he wasn't going to push. He was a patient man, even when it came to his love life.

Lance looked down, then back at Monty. "Goodnight. And thanks for the company."

Monty waved and turned so he wouldn't be even more tempted to steal a kiss. Lance hadn't given him many cues that he was interested, although that might be because Monty couldn't read them. He wasn't exactly the most experienced man in the world when it came to flirting with guys, and he didn't want to embarrass himself or Lance by asking.

So he left. He needed to get home anyway. He wanted to open the clinic as early as possible in the morning, and that meant going to bed at a decent hour. It was already too late for that, but he could still get five or six hours of sleep if he hurried.

Of course, he was sidetracked.

He turned onto the street where his house was, and almost collided with a man running toward him. His messenger bag slipped from his shoulder, and he scrambled to grab it since his computer was in it. Two hands shot toward him along with his, and he breathed easier when they caught it.

"Thank you," he said, looking at the man he'd bumped into.

The man held the bag out for Monty to take. "I'm sorry. I should have looked where I was going. Are you okay?"

"Of course." Monty took the bag and hung it onto his shoulder again. "It was nothing." The man had been running—his t-shirt was damp, and he smelled of sweat and salt, of the night air and of something that had to be him. "I'm Monty."

The man smiled. He was even more gorgeous when he smiled, and Monty hadn't thought that would be possible. "I'm Matthew, but everyone calls me Matt." He held his hand out, frowned, and rubbed it against his stomach. "Sorry. I'm sweaty."

Monty wanted to rub him, and he didn't even care about the sweat. Matt was tall and had wide shoulders Monty could easily imagine clutching in bed.

He shook his head. "That's fine. I need to take a shower anyway. Long day." He took Matt's hand and shook it. "Montague, but everyone calls me Monty. Actually, I usually beg people to call me Monty."

Matt chuckled. "I can see that. Montague is a mouthful."

"It is." Monty and Matt both dropped their hands.

Monty knew he should head home, but he found he'd rather stay where he was and talk to Matt. He wasn't sure why, but then, the entire evening had been weird, first with Lance, then with Matt. "Late evening run?" he asked.

Matt grinned. "I had to. I'm staying with friends right now, and they're having sex. Loud sex."

Monty grimaced. "I see."

"Yeah. It's not something I want to imagine, even though, well." He waved. "Never mind. What about you? You're not running, and from your bag, it looks like you just left work."

"No. Well, I did leave work late, but I had a chat with a

friend."

Matt looked around. "Want me to walk you home? I know the town is mostly safe, but I'd feel better if I knew you weren't alone roaming the streets."

Monty arched a brow. "This isn't the first time I've walked around alone late at night, and it won't be the last."

"Still."

"And what about you? You'd have to run home alone once you saw me to my door."

Matt shrugged. "I'm a detective. I can take care of myself."

"I see." Monty gestured toward the street. "I live that way."

"So do my friends. After you, Monty."

Monty wasn't sure what to do. He didn't have to do anything, but he was confused, and he hated being confused. He liked Lance, but he also liked Matt, probably more than he should in either case. Lance had a huge job in DC, and Matt clearly wasn't from Hope. Hope didn't even have a police station yet. "Who are your friends? I probably know them if we live on the same street."

"Sully, Keating, and Rodrick."

The throuple. "I do know them." Everyone did. They'd been much talked about when they'd moved to Hope, not because they were a throuple but because Keating was a white tiger shifter. People had soon realized he was just like everyone else. Monty liked him, and his two men, although Sully was somewhat hard to get to know. "Are you a shifter like them?" Monty doubted it, since Matt had said he was a detective, although it wouldn't be unheard of for a shifter to manage to pass as human. It was hard, but not impossible.

"Nope. I'm human. You're a shifter, though, right?"

"A fox shifter. Can I ask how you met them? You have to be good friends to be staying with them."

Matt rubbed the back of his neck. "Sully and I met in the city, in a bar. We were involved for a while, before he, Rodrick, and Keating decided to give it a try. I helped the pack as much as I could back then, and now that the three of them live here, they invited me to spend some time with them during my vacation."

"And how do you like Hope?" Monty was curious about a human's point of view on the town. All the humans he knew, minus Lance, of course, lived there and were involved in relationships with shifters. There were human visitors, but Monty always gave them a wide berth, just in case.

"It's nice. Quiet. Quieter than what I'm used to anyway."

"Is that a good thing?"

"Oh, yeah. I love my job, but I'm ready for a change."

"A change? Are you going to move?"

"I don't know anything for sure for now." Matt smiled at Monty. "But I like it here. The town is cute, and the people are nice." He looked Monty up and down. "Very nice."

Monty smiled back. How could he not? He might be a mess of emotions and questions, but he wasn't going to put a stop to this. He'd never cared about conventions, and to him, the thought that a relationship had to be between a man and a woman was ridiculous. He'd been lucky to find a pack that didn't care that he preferred men, and he'd had some relationships over the years, although not since he'd moved to Hope.

He could easily see himself with Lance, and he could see himself with Matt just as easily. That left him with a choice — or maybe not. What if they thought the same way he did? Matt clearly didn't have a problem with throuples. If anything, Monty could maybe bring it up to the two of them and see what they thought of it.

He didn't want a hook-up, with either of them. He'd lived uncertainly for too long, always afraid of being caught and killed, always wondering if today was his last day.

He didn't want to do that anymore. He'd gotten used to the thought that he was safe now, that he'd probably have a long life, and he didn't want to live it alone. And if he was lucky enough to get both the men he wanted, then he'd grab that chance with both hands.

ABOUT THE AUTHOR

Catherine lives in Italy, country of good food and hot men. She used to write fantasy as a child, but it was reading her first gay erotic romance novel that made her realize that that was what she really wanted to write.

After graduating from college in English language and translation, she divides her day between writing, reading, taking care of her son and reading some more.

You can find her on Facebook and Twitter or on her website: authorcatherinelievens.wordpress.com

Email: lievens.catherine@gmail.com

Newsletter: http://eepurl.com/c-uvKn